The Secret Mission

Huguenot Inheritance Series #2

The Secret Mission

A Huguenot's Dangerous Adventures in the Land of Pesecution

(Based on historical facts)

by

A. VAN DER JAGT

**INHERITANCE PUBLICATIONS
NEERLANDIA, ALBERTA, CANADA
PELLA, IOWA, U.S.A.**

National Library of Canada Cataloguing in Publication Data

Van der Jagt, A. (Anton), 1921-
  The secret mission

  ISBN 0-921100-18-3

  1. Huguenots—Fiction. 2. France—Fiction. II. Title.
PR9130.9.J34S4 2001   823'.914   C2001-911070-7

Library of Congress Cataloging-in-Publication Data

Van der Jagt, A. (Anton), 1921-
  The secret mission : a Huguenot's dangerous adventures in the land of
persecution (based on historical facts) / A. van der Jagt.
     p. cm. — (Huguenot inheritance series ; #2)
Sequel to: The escape.
Summary: John Dubois returns to France on a secret mission of the Dutch
government, and while there he tries to find his father.
  ISBN 0-921100-18-3
  [1. Huguenots—Fiction. 2. France—Fiction. 3. Fathers—Fiction.] I.
Title. II. Series.
  PZ7.V28385 Se 2001
  [Fic]—dc21
                                                          2001003582
Cover Illustration: Clair Roza-Bosma

Published by Inheritance Publications
Box 154, Neerlandia, Alberta Canada T0G 1R0
Tel. & Fax (780) 674 3949
Web site: http://www.telusplanet.net/public/inhpubl/webip/ip.htm
E-Mail inhpubl@telusplanet.net

Published simultaneously in U.S.A. by Inheritance Publications
Box 366, Pella, Iowa 50219

Available in Australia from Inheritance Publications
Box 1122, Kelmscott, W.A. 6111 Tel. & Fax (089) 390 4940

Printed in Canada

To Elizabeth, my wife,

source of my inspiration and perseverance

with love and gratitude.

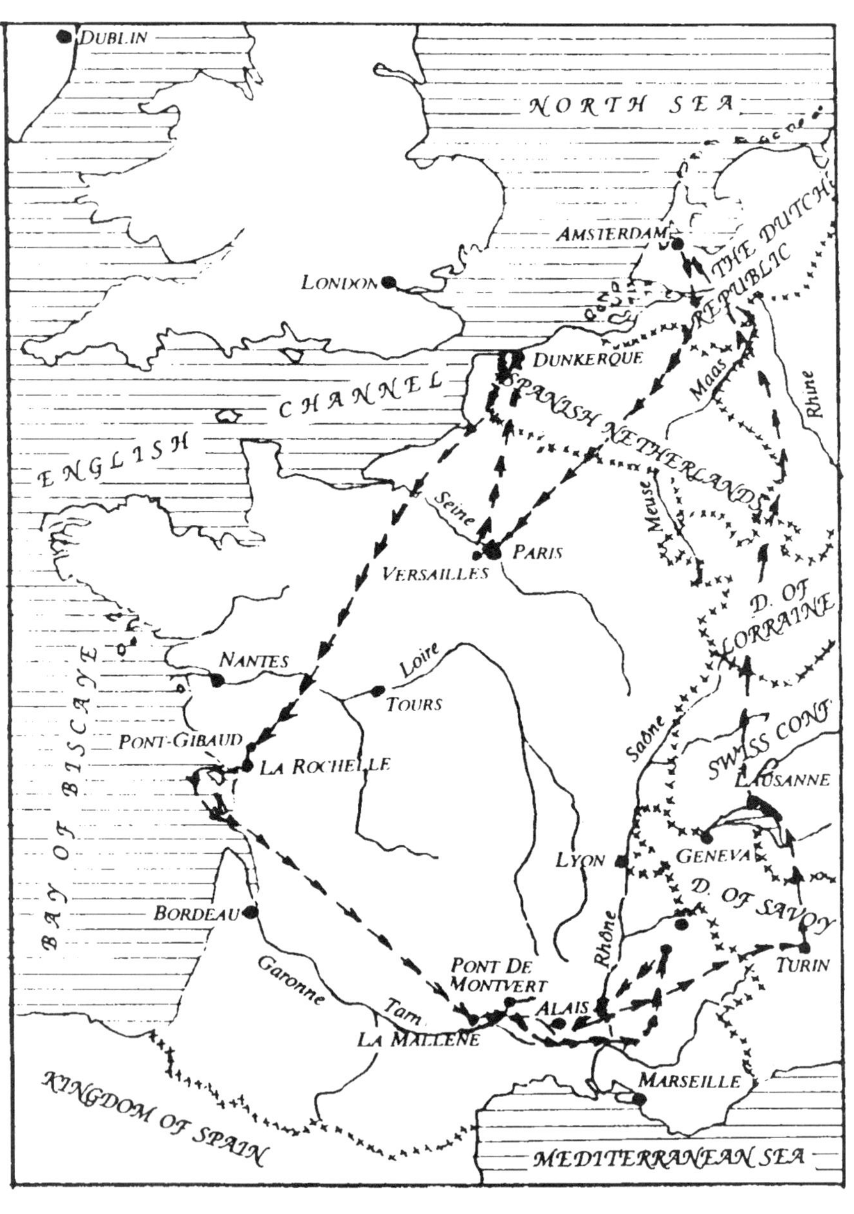

DUBLIN
NORTH SEA
AMSTERDAM
THE DUTCH REPUBLIC
LONDON
DUNKERQUE
Maas
Rhine
CHANNEL
SPANISH NETHERLANDS
ENGLISH
Seine
Meuse
PARIS
VERSAILLES
D. OF LORRAINE
NANTES
Loire
TOURS
Saône
SWISS CONF.
PONT-GIBAUD
LAUSANNE
LA ROCHELLE
BAY OF BISCAYE
LYON
GENEVA
D. OF SAVOY
BORDEAU
Rhône
Garonne
PONT DE MONTVERT
TURIN
Tarn
ALAIS
LA MALLENE
MARSEILLE
KINGDOM OF SPAIN
MEDITERRANEAN SEA

Table of Contents

Table of Illustrations

JOHN PROMOTED

FOOTSTEPS echoing in the hallway disrupted the usual quiet atmosphere of the office of Mr. De Groot, one of the most influential merchants in Amsterdam, the largest city of the Dutch Republic.[1] The steps halted a moment, then the door opened, and a sturdy man entered carrying a large, flat package in his hand.

"This missive is from Mr. Heinsius[2] in The Hague for Mr. De Groot and must be given into his hands immediately," he said aloud to nobody in particular. The four clerks, very much involved in their work, raised their heads and looked a moment at the visitor before continuing their writing, knowing that John would take care of the letter because Mr. Goudriaan, Mr. De Groot's secretary, had not come in yet. John, hired to help Mr. Goudriaan, knew the importance of government letters. He stopped writing, placed the goose feather he was using in a small cup next to the inkpot, and stood up.

"Please give it to me," he said. "I'll take it directly to Mr. De Groot. You can wait in the kitchen at the other end of the hallway. I'll let you know if Mr. De Groot wants you to take a reply back to Mr. Heinsius."

"No, young master," the man replied politely. "I can't wait because I must deliver another message to the City Council. However, I'll drop in later in the afternoon before I return to The Hague. If you have any mail ready for Mr. Heinsius, I'll take it with me then."

---

[1] The Dutch Republic = the United Provinces = the Netherlands, sometimes called Holland, is the oldest republic in western civilization.

[2] Antonius Heinsius (1641-1720) was at the time of this story in 1702, the Grand Pensionary of the Dutch government (comparable to a Prime Minister in modern times). He was especially responsible for the Dutch foreign policy.

The man handed the missive to John and left the office without waiting for John's answer. Special messengers from the government were always in a hurry!

A few steps brought John into a spotlessly clean hallway that led to Mr. De Groot's private office. He knocked softly on the door and waited until called in. Mr. De Groot was sitting behind a large table covered with letters and other papers. He did not like interruptions during his work, but when he saw that a letter from the government had arrived he hastened to remove the seals, and the last thing John saw before he closed the door was Mr. De Groot unfolding the missive.

After returning to his desk, John picked up his quill, sharpened its tip with a penknife, and continued his writing. It was a pity, he thought, that Mr. Goudriaan had to stay home so often. He was getting old and his health was beginning to fail. On the spur of the moment, he decided to visit Mr. Goudriaan tonight on his way home to see how he was doing.

It did not make much difference to John if Mr. Goudriaan came to the office or not. He had enough work to keep him busy for several days. A small part of it was just routine office work like that of the other clerks but most of the time he translated Dutch business letters into French, his mother tongue. He was a Huguenot[3] who had fled the severe persecution in France with his sister Manette and his friend Camille.[4]

A few hours later, Mr. De Groot summoned John to his private office by ringing his office bell. He was writing when John entered, but made an inviting gesture to the chair in front of his table.

"Sit down, John. I'll be ready in a few minutes," he said while he continued writing. After having dried the ink on his letter, he folded it, moved it out of his way and eased himself comfortably in his arm chair.

"Well, John, you've been working in my office for three years now. I'm pleased that you took over a large part of Mr.

---

[3] Huguenots were the Protestant (Reformed) Christians in France.

[4] Their story has been told in A. Van der Jagt, *The Escape* (Neerlandia, AB: Inheritance Publications, 1988).

10

Goudriaan's work, now that he has to stay home so often after the stroke he suffered last year. A few weeks ago I instructed him to give you a variety of difficult tasks, which you handled well. Yesterday he told me that the doctor didn't expect him to recover fully from the stroke. He can't work anymore and must retire. It's not easy to replace an excellent worker like him, but he strongly recommended you for this position. I agree. You are, of course, too young to take over all the duties of a secretary, but I think that your excellent knowledge of the French language, and your ability to express yourself in writing makes you well suited for this job. Therefore, you can have it if you like."

"Oh, yes, Sir. Thank you, Sir. I'll do my best, Sir." John, not used to much praise, blushed. It felt like a dream that he, John Dubois, got this incredible promotion. He was elated and became so confused that he barely knew what he said. Mr. De Groot, understanding his excitement, smiled a little while he outlined John's future responsibilities.

"All right, John. Keep in mind that this position is not an easy one. You must still learn a lot. One of your duties will be to come with me on my business trips. Most of our business is with England and France, as you know. It is important for you to learn to speak English fluently. In fact, your Dutch also needs a lot of improvement.

"Tomorrow, you must move into Mr. Goudriaan's room. It's more convenient for me when you are closer to my office. When I receive visitors I want you to be in this room so that you can take notes, if needed. If you have any questions about your duties, see Mr. Goudriaan and ask him. He promised to help you for the time being. You'll get a salary increase of one guilder a week.

"As my secretary you will need to be better dressed than you are now. I've ordered a new suit for you from Mr. Van Buuren, the tailor. He expects you this afternoon to take your measurements. Obviously, you must pay for it. I've arranged with Mr. Van Buuren that you'll pay him at least the amount of your raise each week until your suit is paid off.

"Now, to return to business, Mr. Heinsius asks in his letter today to see him as soon as it is convenient. We'll visit him on Monday, late in the afternoon. Please draft a reply to his missive notifying him of our visit. His messenger can take it back to him after I've signed it. You must make all the arrangements for this trip. Hire a double seat for me and one for yourself in the morning mailcoach at six o'clock. We'll stay in a hotel, *The Golden Lion*, and return the following Tuesday."

He turned again to his papers showing that he considered the interview to be finished. John, understanding that he was supposed to leave, stood up and, after saying goodbye, returned to the general office.

*   *   *

It was a very happy John who came home that night. He saw his sister Manette in the dining room, laying the silverware on the supper table. Her back was turned toward him, and she did not seem to hear him entering the room. All at once a mischievous smile came on his face. Softly, he tiptoed to her, covered her eyes with his hands and whispered in her ear, "Guess who is holding you, Manette?"

"Well, you are, John. Who else?" she replied, laughing.

"Of course it is me, but what do you think I am? Guess again."

"Don't be silly, you are my brother," she replied impatiently, and began to wriggle so that he could not hold on to her any longer.

Suddenly, he turned her around and kissed her on both cheeks. Then he let her go so abruptly that she nearly fell, and, pounding on his chest, yelled excitedly, "The secretary of Mr. De Groot has kissed you, Manette. Didn't you feel it?"

He yelled so loud that Uncle René, the minister of the French Reformed Church in Amsterdam who had adopted them, came from his study, and his wife, Aunt Marguerite, from the laundry room, anxious to find out what was going on. Somewhat calmer now, he told them about his conversation with Mr. De Groot and his promotion to secretary. Before he even finished his story, they understood that he had been promoted and began to smile. Manette and Aunt Marguerite hugged him at the same time, while Uncle René pounded his shoulders and chuckled, repeating several times, "Congratulations, Son!" After the loud excitement had lessened, Aunt Marguerite remarked that John's promotion must be celebrated by a good supper with friends. Saturday would be the best day for it.

"How proud Dad would be if he knew about it. Do you think that we will see him again some time, John?" Manette whispered to John late that night when they were cleaning the dishes in the kitchen. John assured her again, as he had done so often, that some day their father would be released from the war galleys[5] in France to which he was convicted for life because he was a Huguenot.

"Don't give up, Manette. The Lord will take care of him, as he does of all His children. Maybe we'll hear from him soon. It is such a pity that we haven't found out yet on which ship he is rowing. I don't understand why nobody seems to know where he is! You know what, Manette? The Dutch government is trying hard to get more information about the galleys. Maybe they'll be more successful than our friends in church and will discover where he is. Somebody must have seen him somewhere!

---

[5] War galleys were large, low ships rowed by convicts chained to benches. Six men were allotted to each fifteen-foot oar, and were forced to hold a pace set by an overseer with a whistle.

SECRET MISSION TO FRANCE

"NO, Mr. Heinsius, I can't do it. I haven't the proper connections. It is easy enough to take money to Paris. Anyone can do that. Bringing a large sum to the South of France? Forget about it! Delivering it to the Huguenots in Languedoc?[6] Absolutely impossible!" As he spoke, Mr. De Groot calmly took a small, beautifully ornamented box out of his pocket, opened it and took a pinch of snuff.

Mr. Heinsius had been sitting quietly behind a heavy oak table loaded with letters and papers, but hearing the refusal, he jumped up and began pacing the room.

"Listen, Mr. De Groot, you are evading the main issue and you know it! Delivering a large sum of money to the Huguenots isn't the most important thing in the world. If it can't be done, we won't even try it. I am asking for your help in our thirty-year struggle against King Louis XIV of France. We must complete the task for which my master, King William, has worked his whole life. His death four weeks ago[7] has thrown everything in turmoil, and it will take time to unite our allies again. I know his wishes and his plans and will certainly do my utmost to continue his policies."

Mr. De Groot threw up his hands mockingly and interrupted him with a mischievous smile.

"Hear, hear, the Grand Pensionary of the Republic talks about the instructions of his king. You have changed a lot after we went to school together, haven't you?"

---

[6] Languedoc is in the southeast of France where the persecution of the Huguenots was most severe.

[7] March 8, 1702.

Antonius Heinsius (1641-1720)
Grand Pensionary of the Dutch Republic

"I didn't say my king because he wasn't, but, yes, I admire him. Not because he was the King of England but because he was our Prince William of Orange, the Stadtholder who saved our Republic in 1672 when England, France, Munster, and Cologne tried to trample us down," Mr. Heinsius snapped back, but seeing the amused smile on Mr. De Groot's face, he regained his composure.

"Today, the situation is far worse than in 1688 when our brave Prince William used our navy and marines for invading England. His support of the English Protestants forced England to break their covenant with King Louis XIV, which prevented the destruction of the Protestant religion. From then on, the English have always sided with us so that we could keep King Louis well under control.

"Lately, he has become a troublemaker again," Mr. Heinsius continued. "Once more King Louis is trying to extend his power in Europe, but we and our allies, England, Denmark, and a good number of German states, intend to stop him. We are ready! All our preparations are completed! The navy and army are in excellent shape, and all the allies agree that it's time to teach King Louis a lesson. I expect that in another month or so we will send him a Declaration of War!

"As we all know, Louis persecutes the Huguenots relentlessly for their faith in our Lord, Jesus Christ. This war will make matters far worse for them. King William and his wife, Queen Mary, have always supported the French Huguenots, politically as well as financially.[8] The last few months before his death Prince William worried a lot about them. He felt it to be of the utmost importance to keep them informed about the present situation, and to find some ways or means of maintaining support for them.

"I have at present a total of fifty Louis d'Ors[9] available to help the Huguenots. Twenty were given by King William, twenty by our government and the rest by the French Huguenots in Holland. Part of this sum can be used for reimbursement of the expenses, but the rest should be given to a certain Abraham Mazel, one of the leading ministers in Languedoc. Mind, as I mentioned before, the money is not the most important issue. Informing the Huguenots about the coming war and finding a way to keep in contact with them is far more urgent. I know that you have some dealings with the Huguenots, and therefore I called you to discuss the situation. I hoped, and still hope, that you can and will advise me on how to proceed."

"Well, I can't at this moment," Mr. De Groot replied thoughtfully. "It's certainly impossible to send a common messenger because he'll be jailed as soon as war breaks out. It seems to me that this calls for a government official to be sent to France with a special message, but that wouldn't help either because he wouldn't be allowed to go to the South of France."

"Oh, yes, a smart man might arrange that," Mr. Heinsius replied confidently. "A few months ago, I received a secret missive from the Minister of Finances in France. I think that

---

[8] Queen Mary paid the salaries of several Huguenot ministers in France, Switzerland, and Germany, amongst others.

[9] Fifty Louis d'Ors (50 golden Louis) was equivalent to three years wages for a skilled laborer.

*William of Orange, (1650-1702) King of England
and Stadtholder of the Dutch Republic*

we could use it as an excuse to go to the Huguenots in Languedoc. Wait. Let me get it." He searched through a large pile of letters, took one out and handed it to Mr. De Groot, who read it thoroughly.

"Hmm, I didn't realize their economy had suffered so much after so many Huguenots fled the country,"[10] Mr. De Groot remarked. "The silk industry, the tanneries, and the clothing manufacturing are nearly completely liquidated! I can see that he is worried and would like the return of the Dutch cloth workers and skilled Huguenots."

Suddenly Mr. De Groot began to laugh, but when the Pensionary showed his impatience, not understanding the reason for his mirth, he stopped laughing and explained his thoughts.

---

[10] The industry, put in excellent shape by the previous Minister of Finance, Colbert, was completely ruined by the loss of the Huguenots. The skilled Dutch cloth workers, who had been persuaded by Colbert to settle in Abbeville, left in a body and the industry in the region was extinguished. They enjoyed complete freedom of religion, but they stated that they couldn't stand the persecution of the Huguenots. At Tours, only four thousand workers (one hundred looms) in the silk industry remained out of forty thousand (eight thousand looms). Of the four hundred tanneries in Lorraine, only fifty-four remained. The population of Nantes was reduced from eighty thousand to less than forty thousand.

"Forgive me, Mr. Heinsius. That minister must be a fool to expect us to return the Huguenots in Holland to the slaughterhouse in France." Both men laughed contemptuously.

"I never replied to this letter," Mr. Heinsius said reflectively, "because I don't understand it. Everybody knows that King Louis won't stop the persecution. Either the letter was written without the knowledge of the king or it's some kind of trap."

"True, but it's also an excellent excuse for us to send a special envoy," Mr. De Groot said. "He can officially negotiate terms for their return. At the same time, he could suggest that some convicted Huguenots in France may be willing to cooperate, provided their government is willing to negotiate relaxation of the persecution. Our argument is, of course, that since they trust us we could perhaps influence them more than the French government. If the minister accepts that, our envoy may even get permission to discuss with the Huguenots their conditions in return for their cooperation in the industry. Then he has an excellent excuse to go to the South of France where most of the Huguenots live. When he is there, it should be easy to find the means to forward the money to the proper person."

"Ha, it's a magnificent joke to give the Huguenots more money with their own government unknowingly helping us," Mr. Heinsius said, and both men began to laugh again.

"Let me explain something else," Mr. De Groot continued after they were serious again. "While we were talking, it dawned on me that the solution to your problem may also solve my problem. Let me explain, please. I've a friend, a banker in France who has always been willing to cash my letters of credit[11] and give the money to the Huguenot galley slaves. Lately, I got the impression that some irregularities have occurred. I didn't know how to straighten it out because I can't discuss it in a regular letter. Well, maybe we can work together. I'm willing to act as a special envoy to Paris on government business using your letter as an excuse. If I'm allowed to travel to the South of France, I certainly will find a way to go to Dunkerque[12] where my friend, the banker, lives."

---

[11] A letter of credit = a letter of exchange. Today it is called an international cheque.

[12] In 1662 King Louis XIV purchased Dunkerque (Dunkirk), an important harbor in the Spanish Netherlands, for £400,000.

"Our plan is undoubtedly worth trying," Mr. Heinsius declared. "I think that it is also quite safe. Tomorrow I'll give you an official introduction to the Minister of Finance in Paris. Is that all you need?"

"I'll take my secretary with me," Mr. De Groot replied. "I'll also need official papers for him. He is a French Huguenot, so it is better not to use his real name. Let me think a moment. Yes, his family name is Dubois. His family has lived for many generations in the forest. We can just translate his name in Dutch. Make his papers out in the name of John Van het Woudt.[13] As far as the money for the Huguenots is concerned, I'll take it with me. If I can deliver it, I'll do it. If not, I'll return it to you."

"Excellent! I'll order one of my servants to contact your secretary for the information needed for the official papers. They'll be made up as soon as possible and brought to your house. Obviously, the Republic will reimburse you for all your costs.

"One more thing, Mr. De Groot," he added, looking serious. "Make sure you don't get trapped when the war begins. They have no scruples and would be willing to put you into the Bastille,[14] as they threatened me once.[15] I'll order our ambassador to notify you secretly of the Declaration of War one day before he gives it to King Louis."

Mr. Heinsius then sat down on a corner of the table, and addressed his friend in a more leisurely way.

"Well, Mr. De Groot, our government certainly appreciates your taking care of this assignment. I hope that you don't have to return home today because my dear wife is anxious to have you stay for supper, and of course, we hope that you'll also spend the night in our home!"

*   *   *

One week later, Mr. De Groot and his secretary, John Van het Woudt, traveled to Paris with the regular mail coach.

---

[13] Dubois (French) = Van het Woudt (Dutch) = "of the forest."

[14] State prison in Paris, notorious for the great number of political prisoners who had to spend most of their life there, often without any legal process, forgotten by nearly everyone.

[15] Historical fact.

3

A NASTY ENCOUNTER

IT was late in the afternoon. All day long the weather had been marvelous. Every once in a while the bright sun hid behind some light clouds so that the temperature remained at a comfortable level, just right for walking in the park of the king's palace in Versailles. A lot of people seemed to agree because many of them were still strolling along its lanes.

A large crowd was gathered in front of the palace watching the continuous stream of carriages that brought the noblemen, most of them accompanied by their ladies. The onlookers, mainly servants, footmen, grooms, chambermaids, and people who intended to petition the king or a highly placed official, never tired of seeing the court ritual practiced by these lords. Even before the coach stopped, the footman would jump down from his standing place at the rear of it. He would hurriedly open the door and place a wooden step on the ground. Next, the nobleman would get out, supported by the footman if he was old. As soon as he stood on the ground, he would turn around, bow to his lady, and give her a hand to help her descend. When she was standing on the ground, the lord would offer the lady his arm and both of them would walk in stately decorum to the open palace doors.

John watched the scene for a little while, but soon became tired of it. He turned and walked leisurely along the lanes of the beautiful, landscaped park, enjoying himself tremendously. Traveling was fun, he thought, but he corrected himself immediately. Traveling was not fun, but staying at a place like this park was pleasant.

Sitting for hours between two other passengers on a hard seat in a mailcoach was tiring and certainly not a pleasure. Now he understood why Mr. De Groot always paid for two seats for himself. One seat would be too small for such a broad man as he was.

Every night they had stayed at an inn, but that wasn't fun either. None of these lodgings were clean and some of them were certainly very dirty. He had been glad when at last they had arrived in Versailles.

They were staying in the house of the Dutch ambassador, a somewhat pompous but friendly man. Mr. De Groot had discussed with the ambassador at length the purpose of his unexpected visit. John, being Mr. De Groot's secretary, had to attend these discussions. He knew now that the official purpose of this journey was the possible return of the Dutch cloth workers, but that the secret goal was to encourage the Huguenots in the South of France to persevere, and to deliver a large sum of money to them.

After the ambassador had agreed with Mr. De Groot about their approach to the Minister of Finance, Seigneur[16] de Pontchartrain, he had requested an audience with the Minister.

The first two meetings with Seigneur de Pontchartrain and his aide had been boring, and, as far as John was concerned, failures. The Minister had used this opportunity to state that he was displeased with the Dutch government because it hadn't kept his missive secret, and had refused to order the return of the Dutch cloth workers. The Dutch ambassador had apologized, and had tried without success to discuss possible visits of Mr. De Groot to convicted Huguenots with the purpose of finding skilled Huguenot cloth workers.

The third meeting on the day before yesterday had begun in the same way, but the whole atmosphere changed drastically when the Dutch ambassador suddenly flew in a rage. John smiled when he recalled the harsh language he had used to express

---

[16] Seigneur = Sir.

his contempt for the Minister's attitude. Anyway, it had worked! Seigneur de Pontchartrain, astonished to hear such undiplomatic language in his own room, had all at once agreed to negotiate. A lively discussion had filled the rest of the afternoon. In fact, the conversation was sometimes so confused with everyone talking at the same time, that John just couldn't keep up with taking notes.

The outcome was that Seigneur de Pontchartrain refused flatly to give Mr. De Groot permission to travel in France. However, at the end of the afternoon, he turned suddenly to the ambassador, and with a smile suggested in his nasal voice that he would be willing to permit John to go to Dunkerque, the closest city where Huguenots were used as galley slaves. John could question the Huguenots as well as Mr. De Groot, he stated. Taken by surprise, Mr. De Groot had accepted his recommendation, and Seigneur de Pontchartrain had promised to forward an official recommendation to the Dutch consulate for John, so that he could travel without being delayed by zealous officials.

John was elated. He had not mentioned to Mr. De Groot that he was determined to locate his father. This unexpected turn of events gave him an excellent opportunity to question the Huguenots on a war galley about his father. Surely, these Huguenot convicts would know where he might be!

Deep in thought, John had left the more crowded parts of the park, and was now strolling toward its rear. The lanes were still well kept, but here fewer people were enjoying the beautiful landscape.

Suddenly, he became aware that a priest at the other side of the lane halted and watched him closely with a deep frown on his forehead. Before John could react to this unexpected scrutinizing by a stranger, the man crossed over to him and firmly grasped his arm. Shocked, John recognized his Uncle Francis, who held him in a tight grip, the same uncle who had denounced his father to be a Huguenot so that he was convicted for life to a rower's seat on one of the war galleys.[17]

---

[17] See *The Escape*.

"You must be John, the son of my dear brother, John Dubois," Father Francis exclaimed. "You look exactly like him when he was your age. What are you doing here? I thought that you had gone abroad."

"Oh, I'm just working, Uncle Francis," John replied, wondering if he could escape the clutching hand on his arm.

"I'm happy to see you," Uncle Francis replied with his face close to John's. "To be honest, I'm surprised to see you walking in the king's garden. When did you repent and become a Roman Catholic again? Or are you still a Huguenot?

"Why don't you answer?" he added with a venomous glow in his eyes when John didn't reply directly. "Oh, yes, I know the answer. You are as stubborn as your father. You haven't repented, right?"

"No, I'm still a Huguenot, Uncle Francis," John answered boldly. Having recovered from the shock of seeing his uncle, he tried to shake his grip off. "It's none of your business, though!"

"None of my business, eh?" Uncle Francis cried. "You'll know better soon. Come with me to the guard house." He grabbed John's other arm also, and tried to turn John around in the direction of the palace. John struggled vehemently to free himself, but his uncle held on to him and yelled to a few passers-by, "Help, help bring this scoundrel to the guardhouse!"

Several men, some of them soldiers, curiously turned toward them to see what was going on. When they saw that a priest was involved in a fight, they hurried to help Uncle Francis. John, terribly scared when he saw them coming, managed just in time to free his right arm, and with a large swing hit his uncle in the face. His uncle involuntarily released his hold on the other arm slightly. John felt it, and instantaneously tore this arm loose. Uncle Francis didn't give up, though, and tried to grab John's arm again.

John, seeing that he ran the danger of being hemmed in between Uncle Francis and the other men, did not take that risk. He swung his fist again and hit his Uncle Francis directly on the nose. At the same time, he turned around, and seeing that one of the passers-by was close enough to grab him, suddenly

. . . with a large swing hit his uncle in the face.

jumped sideways, dove underneath the arms of another man, and raced across a small grass plot. He fought his way through several bushes, turned past a few trees and had, he thought, shaken the men off. The danger was not over yet, so he kept running as fast as possible through small bushes, across flowerbeds, and green lawns until he had completely lost his way.

After a while, he was quite sure that his pursuers must have given up the chase because he heard no alarming sounds. He slackened his pace while he was crossing a large, grassy field to get his breath. At the other side he stood still, looking backwards. After a few moments, he saw the bushes moving and two men appeared, wearing the uniforms of foot soldiers. They had seen John and with a triumphant yell they raced across the field toward him. Of course John didn't wait for them, but turned and began to run again through the bushes. He felt, however, that he couldn't keep up with the chase much longer. He was extremely tired, and needed all his willpower to keep his feet moving. Any moment now he might have to give up.

At the very moment that he was ready to surrender, he came out of the bushes, and saw a very large building separated from him by several flowerbeds, footpaths, and fountains with sculpture groups. He recognized it as the Grand Trianon, the mansion King Louis XIV had built and liked best. It was the last place where he wanted to go because he expected that many of the people in front of the mansion might try to catch him if his pursuers yelled for help. He did not have any choice, though, and continued to run as fast as he could in a straight line toward the palace, through flower beds and across grass plots. He wasn't even halfway, when he heard his pursuers yell. A quick glance backward showed him that they couldn't run fast either.

When he came closer to the mansion, he saw that he was approaching its rear where only a few people were walking, mostly at the farthest end. He slowed down, at a loss where to go next. The wall of the mansion contained many sculptures, beautiful arches, large windows, and many heavy carved doors. It would be foolish to walk through one of these doors, he thought. Most likely they would be guarded by soldiers, and if not, he just could not take the risk that his pursuers would find him while he was interrogated by somebody at the entrance.

He continued, slower now, walking along the wall watching for any opportunity to hide himself. Suddenly, he saw under one of the arches a small, rather insignificant-looking door, half hidden behind a staircase. It looked like an entrance for the servants to enter the palace unobtrusively. Instinctively, he opened it, went inside and closed the door behind him. He stood in a dimly lit, short hallway, with a heavy oak door at the end and two lighter doors at the sides. It took only a few seconds to discover that the door through which he had come could not be locked. Very much afraid that the soldiers might come in at any moment, he hurriedly tried the side doors, but found

Louis XIV, King of France (1638-1715)

that they were also locked. His last chance was the heavy oak door at the end of the hallway. If that was locked also, he would be trapped, an easy victim for his pursuers.

He darted through the hallway to the end door and turned its knob. It was not locked. He opened it and without looking, hurried through, closing the door behind him.

The scene before his eyes was so unexpected that he remained standing, not knowing what to do next. He stood in a very large room, so spacious and beautiful that the people in it seemed dwarfed and insignificant in comparison. Yet, they were not! They were noblemen and ladies, magnificently dressed. Some of them were walking around, conversing in low voices with each other, several of them were sitting on exquisitely carved oaken chairs, also talking or engaged in playing cards. Everywhere he saw servants, quietly bringing trays with glasses and snacks.

He noticed that nobody paid any attention to him. It flashed through his mind that, dressed as the secretary of Mr. De Groot, the servants would not expect him to be one of their equals, and that the noblemen would consider it below their dignity to give him any attention. Hurried steps in the hallway behind him made him aware of his pursuers, who were doggedly following him. The knowledge that they might open the door any moment now terrified him. His only chance was to move away without drawing attention. He felt that the best thing to do was to act as if he belonged in the room.

He forced himself to walk slowly along the wall of the room, repeating to himself, "Don't rush! Act calmly! Don't run!" It was nerve wrecking to walk so slowly when any minute the soldiers could enter the room. Happily, he came very soon to a solid oak door. Without hesitating, he opened it and walked through. He expected to come into another hallway, but he was wrong. He stood alone in a rather small room with solid oak furniture. When he hurriedly closed the door behind him, he heard a loud noise in the large room. The soldiers had thrown open the other door and jumped into the room. The last thing John saw was the annoyed expressions on the faces of a few lords who were so rudely interrupted in their distinguished conversations.

John expected them to search for him in this room also, and in desperation he looked for a place to hide.

A large, rectangular table stood in the center of the room, surrounded by ten chairs. For a brief moment he considered hiding under the table, but rejected that idea. It was too easy to find him there. The room had large windows and heavy curtains, but no hiding place as far as he could see.

Suddenly, the huge, open fireplace drew his attention. It was a familiar sight because some of the old large houses in Amsterdam also had them. These enormous chimneys often had an iron stepladder imbedded inside for cleaning purposes. He hastened to the chimney and saw the lowest steps of the ladder. Carefully, he went inside without disturbing the woodblocks neatly piled on the grating, and began to climb up without making any noise. Just in time! He had barely gone a few steps when the door opened and somebody said, "This door is open, but nobody is here! I told you that we never saw him. You must be dreaming to think that a criminal would hide in this room. There is just no place to hide, but let's have a look anyway."

He heard some people walking around, but they disappeared soon, after expressing their disappointment in not having found him.

Slowly, he climbed a few steps higher, making sure that he could not be easily seen. After some experimentation, he discovered that by having one foot on a step, his knee two steps higher, and his back against the wall he could bear the strain for a long time. It was difficult to take off his jacket in the narrow, soot-covered channel, but he managed to do it. He rolled the jacket up and let his knee rest on it. He was sure that he could stay for hours in the chimney, if needed.

Now, at last he had time to think of his narrow escape, and a song of thankfulness welled up in his heart to his Father Who had protected him from the hands of his uncle.

*   *   *

At the end of that particular day, Father Francis was sitting on a simple chair in a small room of the house of a fellow priest who had offered him shelter. He had a bleeding nose and a black eye, both of them proof that John knew how to use his fists efficiently. On a low table next to him stood a bowl filled with water, which he used to wet the compresses he placed on his hurt face.

He was furious. He had gone to Versailles to get the support of Père Lachaise,[18] the Jesuit confessor of the king. Long ago, Père Lachaise had been one of his peers at seminary. After John,

---

[18] Père Lachaise (Father Lachaise, 1624-1709) was the priest who was authorized to hear the confessions of King Louis XIV. He gained a very large influence over the king, and encouraged the persecution of the Huguenots.

his nephew, had outsmarted him by fleeing to Amsterdam Father Francis had suffered because of it. The bishop did not want to see him anymore, and he had no chance at all to be promoted to a larger city. At last, he was so fed up with the attitude of the bishop that he had traveled all the way to Paris for his petition. He had arrived yesterday, and his encounter with John was absolutely unexpected. He hated that boy, and realized that catching him would have brought him into good favor with Père Lachaise. However, John had escaped! A few hours later, two soldiers in the guardhouse had told him of their futile pursuit. They said that John had most likely found a hiding place in the Grand Trianon, but nobody knew where. Thinking it over, Father Francis ground his teeth together. He had been outsmarted again by a simple boy!

He wondered why John was in Paris. He recalled that he was decently dressed, and might be in the service of one of the noblemen. If that was true, not everything was lost. One of these days he hoped he might discover him again. In the meantime, it would be better not to talk about it. There would be time enough for that after John was caught.

4

A SURPRISING DISCOVERY

AFTER John had settled as well as possible inside the chimney, he became so nervous all at once and had so many confusing thoughts that he had to clamp his teeth together to keep from crying out loud. He calmed himself by first reciting a few Psalms, and then by forcing himself to think about nice things, like Manette, Uncle René and Aunt Marguerite, and his work. At last he felt calm enough to direct his attention toward the present situation.

His first thought was a feeling of regret that his new, beautiful suit would be ruined by the soot of the chimney. He had been so proud of it, and he could hardly afford another new one. He wondered if it could be cleaned, but then he grinned suddenly. What a fool he was to think of such insignificant things while he was trapped in a tight spot! It would be better to find out how to get out of the mansion and safely to the consulate.

For the time being, he could not do anything and must stay where he was. The people in the large room next door would probably not leave until late at night and as long as they were there, he must stay put. At least he didn't have to walk the streets in daylight with a dirty face, hands, and clothing from the soot of the chimney.

He must have dozed in spite of his awkward position because he suddenly became aware that it was dark outside. When he looked down, he could not distinguish anything at all. Looking up he saw a tiny part of the sky with a few stars.

After having waited a long time in the dark, he decided to go down and listen at the door for any people who might still be in the large room. However, he kept waiting, afraid that it would not be safe as yet. At last he felt that waiting longer would be ridiculous and changed his position to descend the chimney. At that very moment the door opened and some people came in with lamps or candles in their hands. They did not talk to each other so John did not know who or what they were.

While they were in the room, they seemed to light the large candle holder John had seen hanging above the oaken table. The room became so well illuminated that John could even see all the details of the firewood lying on the grate. They sounded like servants who had to prepare the room for a meeting. After they had left, he made himself more comfortable, and waited patiently for the things to come.

A short time later, the door opened again, and two people walked in. They talked in low voices about the excellent supper they had enjoyed. The chimney apparently carried the sound well because John could understand them and heard from their talk that they were Père Lachaise and Mr. Chamillart, the Minister of War. Two more people entered somewhat later. John recognized the nasal voice of Seigneur de Pontchartrain. The other one was addressed as the Marquis de Torcy, the Minister of Foreign Affairs. They talked casually about people and events John had never heard of, but they became silent when the door opened again.

"Gentlemen, His Majesty, the Sun King, the Grand Monarch will attend this meeting." John had not heard this voice before, but later discovered that it was from the Duc de Beauvilliers, the special councillor of the king.

"Good evening, gentlemen," an agreeable voice said, followed by the reply of the others, "Good evening, Your Majesty," and, "At your service, Your Majesty."

With a shock, John realized that it must be King Louis XIV himself who had a secret meeting with his principal advisers. Frightened, he understood that it made his position extremely dangerous. His life was at stake if he was discovered. The least they would do would be to lock him up in the Bastille for life, or even to have him killed right away in secret. In a silent prayer, he asked for the Lord's protection in this precarious situation.

"Well, let's sit down and begin our discussion," the king said, sounding somewhat impatient. John heard chairs moving and then the Marquis de Torcy brought up the issue of the Great Alliance of England, The Netherlands, Denmark, and some German states. A lively discussion followed among all but the king, who remained silent most of the time. John gathered that they expected the war to start, but not soon. Other issues followed. Frequently, John knew too little to understand the importance of the different arguments. He did his utmost, however, to memorize as much as possible. After a long time, the participants in the meeting seemed to run out of new issues and John got the feeling that it would soon be over. Suddenly, he heard the voice of Seigneur de Pontchartrain speaking again.

"Your Majesty, I must report one more problem. In line with your orders, I have delayed my discussions with the special

Seigneur de Pontchartrain (1643-1727)

envoy of Holland, Mr. De Groot, as long as possible. In the last meeting the Dutch ambassador forced my hand so that I have given them permission to interrogate the Huguenots on one of our war galleys in Dunkerque. I told him that his secretary could go, but that he was not allowed to travel without our permission. He is too important to let slip through our fingers now that we have him here!

"During our last meeting we agreed that the interrogations are important to us. We know that the Huguenots are receiving financial support from the Dutch, but our spies have been unable to discover the French collaborators whom the Dutch employ. The Huguenots trust the Dutch and their conversations may reveal their middlemen. We may also find Huguenots who are still in hiding. Your Majesty, we need to discuss two more problems. How can we make sure to hear an honest report about the discussions of the Dutch secretary with the Huguenots; and what are we going to do with Mr. De Groot and his secretary after they have served our purpose?"

John nearly betrayed himself by loosening his grip on the iron ladder when he heard these words. At the last moment, he managed to regain his composure without making any noise. He strained his ears so that he wouldn't miss any words of the conversation.

"I certainly don't know why you make a problem of a simple matter," Père Lachaise said contemptuously. "If Your Majesty permits, I will send letters to the chaplains aboard the galleys. They belong to the Lazarists,[19] well known in our church for their zeal. They'll find ways and means to overhear the conversations, I'm sure."

"Yes, I agree," the king replied. "It was smart to keep the envoy here and to send his secretary, who may be easier to deal with than his master. Informing the Lazarists is a simple

---

[19] The order of the Lazarists, in those days usually called "of the mission," was founded by Vincent de Paul, the confessor of the mother of King Louis XIV. They had even more influence than the Jesuits in that time, and were known for their fanaticism. They were cruel persecutors of the Huguenots, and served as chaplains aboard the war galleys.

Père Lachaise (1624-1709)

solution, which I like. As far as the final destination of the envoy and his secretary is concerned, put them in the Bastille. We'll get every ounce of their knowledge out of them, and then we just forget that they exist. Also a simple solution, ha, ha."

Everybody laughed politely with the king.

"I don't think that we have to discuss any other issues, gentlemen. Thank you for coming to this meeting. Good night," the king added. John heard him stand up, followed by the moving of all the other chairs. Somebody opened the door, and they all left the room.

John sighed with satisfaction. He could barely move any more, his feet and knees were so cramped. He waited for some time, expecting a servant to come to extinguish the candles. Nobody came and at last he slowly climbed down.

The room was in disorder. All the chairs were moved around and the table was covered with wine glasses and several empty wine bottles. The candles were burning low in their holders, and some were even burnt out. Seeing the wine glasses, he suddenly felt how thirsty he was. He went to the table and drank some wine that was left over in the bottom of a glass.

After having stretched his arms and legs a few times, he felt somewhat better. His muscles were still aching, and he was strangely tired, but it shouldn't bother him in going to the consulate. He listened at the door. Everything was quiet. It seemed that no one was in the large room. Carefully he opened the door a little and looked through the crack. The room was empty. Some candles were still burning low in their holders, but most of them were extinguished. Slowly, he entered and walked along the wall to the door through which he had entered the room in the afternoon.

He listened at the door, and distinctly heard the voices of some men talking and laughing. Was his way of escape blocked by these men? Did he have to find another exit? The windows couldn't be used. They were too high. The other doors, which were used by the nobility, would be his last recourse but they would be dangerous. In the hallways, he might meet people asking questions, not even considering the possibility that he might lose his way, never having been there. This door to the outside was obviously his best way of escape in spite of the men. He opened the door a crack, looked through it and saw that one of the doors that was closed in the afternoon was now wide open. The men's voices came from that direction.

It would be easy to pass that open door if he made a dash for the end of the hallway as long as it wasn't blocked by somebody. However, the men would hear him, which he didn't like. It would be better to leave secretly without drawing attention. An idea crossed his mind. He would try to tiptoe along the corridor and maybe the men wouldn't hear him.

Without making any noise, he bent over, untied his shoes, took them off, and held them in his hands. Stealthily walking on his toes, he came close to the door, where he crouched down and carefully peeked into the room. It was a bakery in the basement of the Trianon. A very fat man, standing at a large wooden table was kneading dough into loaves of bread with his powerful hands. A line of loaves were on boards ready to put in the oven behind him. At the other side of the bakery, another man was standing in a trough just above the ground, kneading dough with his feet. They were apparently preparing the bread for the next day while they kept a lively conversation going.

John stood up again, waited for a favorable moment when the fat man had turned toward the other one and went noiselessly past the door. He heard the man in the trough saying, "Have a look into the hallway, Armand. I thought that somebody walked by." But before the man could even look into the corridor, John had opened the door and was outside.

It was pitch dark. The stars were hiding behind the clouds, and the moon couldn't be seen either. Hesitantly, John took a few steps forward, felt for the wall at his right side, and let his fingers glide along the bricks. Several steps later his fingers felt that the wall made a right turn, which agreed with the picture he had in his mind of the door entrance. After having gone a few more yards, as he estimated, his fingers felt the wall make another turn to the right. This time he knew he should not follow the wall anymore but must continue in a straight line to reach the road that ran along the back of the Trianon.

It was awkward to walk in the dark without the guidance of the wall, but he kept shuffling along until he felt the hard road surface underneath his feet. He had a good idea where the Trianon was in relationship to the major exits of the park so he knew roughly in which direction to follow the road.

It was important not to deviate from the road, but John figured that out easily enough. He walked with his left foot on the road and his right foot on the grass!

Walking barefoot in the dark at least has the advantage of letting your feet guide you along the road, John thought, smiling. He got so used to this way of walking that he gradually increased his speed without realizing it. Suddenly, he stumbled over a large piece of rock. He tried to keep his balance but failed, and with a loud thud he fell, hitting his head on the ground. Dazed, he lay for several minutes in this position. Then he turned slowly around and sat up, holding his head with both hands until the dizziness disappeared. He wondered why he had been so foolish to try to get to the consulate in the dark. Why not wait until morning?

He felt his way back to the top of the incline and walked carefully away from the road until he felt a large tree with his hands. He sat down and made himself comfortable with his back against the trunk.

It was a beautiful night, cloudy but comfortably warm. Most of the time, he listened to all the noises he knew from his childhood when he lived with his parents in the forest. Every once in a while he dozed off, but woke up often enough to be aware of how far the night had advanced. At last he saw that morning was coming. He could distinguish the trees again. He stood up and walked slowly along the road to the park exit without seeing anyone.

Even there, everything was quiet. The guards had gone inside the guard house, not expecting any visitors at that early hour.

Outside the park, he put his shoes on again and walked slowly toward the consulate, arriving safely an hour later.

He felt for the door knocker and pounded lightly. Nothing happened. He knocked a second time, louder and longer. Still nothing happened. Impatiently, he knocked again, so loudly that the whole house seemed to wake up. He heard doors thrown open, footsteps, and the subdued noise of voices. After having waited far too long, he felt, someone came through the corridor and opened the door a crack.

"Who is there?" a voice asked.

"It is I, John Van het Woudt," John answered, recognizing the voice. "Hurry, Karel. Open the door, please. Don't be a slowpoke." Karel, one of the Dutch servants of the ambassador, barely avoided being hit in the face by the door when John, impatient, suddenly pushed the door wide open and walked in.

"What happened to you, John? Everybody was worried when you didn't show up last night." He raised the lantern he was carrying and looked at John closely, astonished. "What a sight you are! You look like a chimney sweep."

"I need to talk to Mr. De Groot directly," John said, ignoring Karel's inquiry. "Please, wake him up. No, wait a moment. First, I've got to wash myself." He thought a moment and added, "The water in the washbowl in my room is not enough, I need far more. Please, bring a few pitchers of water to my room. Don't wake anyone up." He could feel Karel's reluctance to carry water in the middle of the night and therefore changed his tone of voice.

"Listen, Karel, it is important that nobody knows how dirty I am. I can't say more, but I'm depending on you to keep this secret. See you in my room!" He turned, and went upstairs. When Karel brought the water, he thanked him profusely and dismissed him with a few friendly words suggesting that Karel could go to bed because he would wake up Mr. De Groot himself. As soon as he was alone, he stripped, washed himself thoroughly, and put on his second best suit.

When he was ready, he went to the first floor, where Mr. De Groot slept, and quietly knocked on the door. Mr. De Groot heard him directly, came to the door and asked who was knocking.

"John Van het Woudt, Sir," John answered. "I have important news, and need to discuss it with you immediately, if you please."

"Wait a moment until I've dressed," Mr. De Groot answered.

A short time later, he opened the door and let John in. Without much ado, John related to him everything that had happened. Mr. De Groot was dumbfounded when he heard of the meeting in the room of the Grand Trianon.

"You've heard state secrets that must be told to Mr. Heinsius, the Grand Pensionary, as soon as possible. In the meantime, we are both in great danger, as you told me. The ambassador must be informed immediately. I'll wake him up and discuss the situation with him." He looked at John sharply and began to smile.

"John, wake up. You are sleeping in your chair," he said. John made a real effort to open his eyes, but they kept falling shut.

"All right, John, lie down on my bed. Tomorrow morning we can talk things over just as well," Mr. De Groot said. He helped John to stand up and brought him, still sleeping, to the bed. He gave him a push so that John fell on the blanket where he continued his dreams. Mr. De Groot then left the room to visit the ambassador.

*   *   *

The following morning, Mr. De Groot, the ambassador, and John had a meeting where John again related all the events of the previous day. The ambassador asked several questions, and at last expressed his appreciation for John's actions. He mentioned that he also had news to tell.

"John, I mentioned to Mr. De Groot the latest news, and I think that you deserve to know it also. Yesterday, I received a secret missive from Mr. Heinsius. He instructed me to give King Louis the official Declaration of War today, and then to return to Holland. I discussed it with Mr. De Groot, and we both agree that it can wait one more day, I'll hand over the Declaration tomorrow.[20] The reason for the delay is the safety of both of you. I have other news also. This morning, Seigneur de Pontchartrain forwarded a special permit for you, John, to go to Dunkerque to interrogate the Huguenots. However, I don't think that you should do it under the circumstances and that you had better return to Holland! We prefer to have you in Holland rather than to get lost or jailed in France. Here is the permit. You can read it yourself," he added, handing John a folded parchment.

---

[20] May 15, 1702.

John opened it and glanced over the contents.

I, Louis Phélipeaux, Seigneur de Pontchartrain, etc., Minister of Finance, appointed by His Royal Majesty Louis XIV, King of France, the Sun King, the Grand Monarch, etc., etc., declare that John Van het Woudt, representative of the Dutch Republic, has been assigned to a secret mission by me. As my special envoy, he is allowed to travel freely in France, and to interrogate Huguenot convicts confidentially. Everyone, especially officials in the King's service, must give him any help possible in completing his assignment. Anyone obstructing him in his duty will be severely punished.

    Louis Phélipeaux
    Seigneur de Pontchartrain
    (Minister of Finance)

"I'm very sorry, Sir," John replied politely, while he refolded the permit and put it in his breast pocket, "but I disagree with you. If I don't go, Seigneur de Pontchartrain will certainly have me in prison tomorrow, especially if you are to give him the Declaration of War of our republic. Even if he delayed it a few days, I could meet my Uncle Francis at any time with the same result. On the other hand, if I leave immediately, I'll probably be able to interrogate the Huguenot convicts before any action is taken. At that time, I must be on my guard, but I've a far better chance of escaping if I'm not in Paris. Besides, this passport is an excellent opportunity to find out where my father is. A few of the convicts must know of him and where he might be. I hope that my interrogation will, at least, give me that information and if I find any trace of him, I'll follow it, for sure. If I don't get what I want, I'll find ways and means to continue my search. I've made up my mind that I better now find out if he is still alive for I don't know if I will get another opportunity in the future. I plan to go tomorrow morning at sunrise if I can get your permission, Sir."

Both men had listened quietly. Mr. De Groot explained to the ambassador that John's father was serving a life term on the galleys, but that nobody in Holland knew where he was. After ample consideration, they both agreed that John's plan was acceptable, provided he was very careful.

"I'm wondering, John," Mr. De Groot said reflectively. "Are you willing to take over the rest of my assignment as well and deliver a large sum of money into the hands of a certain Abraham Mazel, one of the Huguenot leaders in Languedoc? Mind, you don't have to do it if you don't like it. We won't blame you if you'd rather not because it's a large responsibility. However, I'll tell you one thing, the Huguenots need this money badly. I dare to ask your help because I know that you have crossed France before when you took your sister to Holland, and you may have to leave again in the same way if you take this assignment."

"I am willing," John said simply. "I know that several ministers have returned to France to serve the Church of our Lord in spite of the danger. If they are willing to risk their life for the Church, so am I!"

"I've one more request, John," Mr. De Groot added. "I'm used to sending money to a banker in Dunkerque who handed it over to the Huguenots on the galleys. His name is Mr. Penetrau. A few months ago, we heard from other sources that he cannot be trusted anymore. It seems that he has tried to keep the money for himself instead of using it to reduce the suffering of our brothers in Christ. If you have a chance, I would appreciate you finding out about it." John agreed about this also, but mentioned that he would like to get more details.

"That's all right," Mr. De Groot replied. "After this meeting we can sit down and go over your plans together."

"Now we have to solve the most difficult problem: how to get you safely out of France, Mr. De Groot," the ambassador stated. "Do you have any suggestions yourself? Of course, I can try to take you with my people, but I'm sure that the king's men will find ways to detain you. They know that you don't belong to my staff, but are a special envoy."

"I've been worrying about what to do, but couldn't dream up any workable scheme," Mr. De Groot complained. "Maybe it would be best to disguise myself and try to walk home. It's a poor solution because my Dutch accent will give me away. Besides, my health isn't good enough for such adventures."

John had listened with a smile on his face, wondering why these men didn't see the solution, which was so evident to him.

"I think that it is very simple," he exclaimed. "The government spies will, obviously, expect Mr. De Groot, the special envoy, to be with the ambassador in Versailles. It is easy to distract their attention away from the consulate. This afternoon the ambassador could deliver a letter from Mr. De Groot to Seigneur de Pontchartrain. In that missive he expresses his regret that his presence is needed urgently in Holland, and that he'll return as soon as possible. That is absolutely true. He is needed in Holland. If that missive is given, the attention of King Louis' spies will be directed to all roads going to Holland, and not to the consulate where Mr. De Groot stays, disguised as one of the common servants. I'm sure that he then could leave with the ambassador after the Declaration of War has been delivered." Both men applauded his solution, and after some discussion were convinced that it would work.

The rest of the day was used in preparation for John's journey. A good riding horse was purchased, and Mr. De Groot gave to John the fifty Louis d'Ors to be delivered to Abraham Mazel. They were packed into a valise, attached to the saddle.

At the end of the day Mr. De Groot had a long talk with John. He described his talk with Mr. Heinsius, and explained the business with Mr. Penetrau, the banker in Dunkerque, in detail. At last he gave John a Letter of Exchange for Mr. Penetrau. When John protested that one or two Louis d'Ors would be plenty enough for his journey, Mr. De Groot smiled.

"You misunderstand the purpose of this Letter of Credit completely. Let me explain. You heard yourself that the French are suspecting the Dutch of sending money for support of the Huguenots. You, as a Dutch envoy, will be watched more closely than anyone else. The same applies for everybody you will be in contact with. It is most unlikely that any government official will search you as long as you can show him your special permit, but we don't like Mr. Penetrau to become a suspect for supplying the money. Therefore, officially, you aren't bringing money at all. You are asking for a large sum of money, forty Louis d'Ors, to be exact, paid for by this Letter of Exchange. Nobody needs to know that you'll use twenty Louis d'Ors, a gift of our ambassador, for the Huguenots on the galleys. The other eighty crowns[21] you will keep for emergencies during your stay in France. If you don't need as much, just give the rest to Abraham Mazel as a special gift. If Mr. Penetrau can be trusted, he will remain our middleman. If you aren't sure, try to find another one."

After John had pocketed the Letter of Exchange, Mr. De Groot showed John another letter, small and sealed with the sign of the Dutch Republic.

"John, I have wondered all night long if you should take this letter to deliver it if possible. Let me explain. When Mr. Heinsius discussed the money that must be delivered to Abraham Mazel, he mentioned that I wouldn't be too far from the French-Savoy border. He wrote this letter and requested me to deliver it if I could. Obviously, it's dangerous to be caught with this letter. On the other hand I know its content. It is certainly worthwhile to take some risk if it can be given into the hand of the Duke of Savoy. You don't have to take it, but I think that you could sew the letter into your coat and try to go to Savoy after you have delivered the money." John accepted this secret part of his mission, also, without hesitation.

The next morning at sunrise John left the consulate, ready for the great adventure.

---

[21] 4 crowns = 1 Louis d'Ors.

5

JOHN'S ARRIVAL IN DUNKERQUE

JOHN reached the city of Dunkerque late in the afternoon five days after he had left the consulate. He rode through the main gate and then followed a narrow street going into the center of the city. The road, poorly paved with many cobblestones missing, was dirty. The houses and shops were shabby and badly in need of a new coat of paint.

"Bah, why don't they clean up that dirty mess," he muttered to himself, guiding his horse carefully around a garbage pile where two dogs were fighting for a large bone.

It did not take long to reach the large square in the city center where the houses were higher and built of brick. It was rather busy, with a lot of people going in different directions, most of them common citizens probably going home after work. The swaggering walk of others betrayed them as being sailors, and the foreign-looking clothes of a few showed them to belong to other nationalities.

John did not stop because he guessed that another twenty minutes would bring him to the harbor where he hoped to see a war galley. He had seen all different kinds of sailing ships in the harbor of Amsterdam, but never a war galley. They were used by the French navy only and generally stayed close to the French coast. He wished fervently that the one on which his father was serving his life term was in the harbor so that he would see him.

Closer to the harbor, the disagreeable stench of outhouses, pigsties, and rotten wood of the city became more and more mixed with the particular odor of seawater and tar common to most coastal harbors. It was exciting to have reached the place where his father might be, or where somebody probably knew

A war galley leaving the harbor.

where he was. He was happy, but also worried. In his heart, he knew that it was foolish to go to the harbor at that time of the day. No decent citizen, particularly not a representative of the Dutch Republic, was supposed to be there at night. It was dangerous, especially for well-dressed foreigners. It was still light, but very soon it would be dark, the perfect time for an attack by robbers.

In this area few common city people were on the street and nearly every house was a tavern where sailors were drinking and brawling. He came to a sudden decision, scolded himself, turned his horse and deliberately began to ride back to the city center. Why would he risk everything by becoming impatient? His plan would fail miserably if he was robbed or even if he was found at the harbor at night. He must use common sense and go to an inn. There was no need to hurry to the harbor.

"I wonder where I can find an inn. It should be somewhere on this road, I think," he muttered. Five minutes later he stopped his horse in front of an old, somewhat shabby-looking brick building, which carried the sign *Auberge du Roi.*

The innkeeper must have a good sense of humor daring to call this rundown lodge the King's Inn, he thought, chuckling, while he dismounted. He threw the reins over a pole in front of the building, unclasped his saddle bag and carried it in his hand, feeling tired and stiff after five days of traveling on horseback.

The door opened into the main room of the inn. Three morose men were sitting at the table, each with a glass of wine, while the innkeeper was pouring a glass of beer for another customer. When John entered, he looked up, hurriedly put the glass down and welcomed John, smiling and bowing.

"Good evening, Sir. What can I do for you, Sir," he asked submissively.

"A good meal, a bed to stay tonight, and somebody to take care of my horse," John answered curtly, remembering that Mr. De Groot had emphasized the importance of being haughty and exacting like all people in his position.

"Yes, Sir. I'm honored. You are welcome, Sir. Please, can you show your tax certificate,[22] Sir?"

"I've nothing to do with your taxes. I'm from Holland with an assignment of His Majesty, King Louis XIV. Here are my credentials." He handed them over to the innkeeper who apparently could not read, for he held them awkwardly upside down.

"I've to show them to the sheriff, Sir, but I'll return them to you tomorrow morning, if you please, Sir."

"No, you don't," John replied, and calmly took the papers out of the hand of the innkeeper. "I told you, I've nothing to do with your taxes. You can tell the sheriff that I'm here and that I desire to see him tonight." The astonished innkeeper, afraid of John's authoritative attitude, did not dare object.

"Yes, Sir. I'll send one of my people directly to the sheriff, Sir."

"My horse needs a thorough grooming. Can you take care of it?" John asked.

"Certainly, Sir. We have a good stable and an excellent stable boy to look after him. I'll show you to your room first, if you

---

[22] If an innkeeper was found guilty of giving a bed to anybody, even a beggar, who had not paid his taxes to the government, he would have to give board and room to a soldier, who would collect the taxes including a large fee for himself.

like, Sir. Please follow me." The innkeeper turned, opened a door behind the counter and ascended a flight of stairs. On the second floor he showed John a small room with a single bed and told him that he could rent it for twenty sous a day, to be paid in advance. John accepted, took his wallet and counted out the rent for one day.

"When can I have supper?" John asked, smelling some cooking aromas.

"Any time, Sir," the innkeeper replied, leaving the room. "Supper is ready and can be served in your room as well as downstairs. Just as you like, Sir."

*   *   *

Less than an hour later, John finished his meal in the large room downstairs. The innkeeper cleaned his table and asked if he needed anything else. He was curious about the business of "that Dutch fellow, who must be a high official."

"Yes," John said, "One of the reasons I came here is to visit Mr. Penetrau on business. What kind of man is he? Do you have somebody to direct me to his house?"

"You mean Mr. Penetrau, the banker? Three of the Penetrau's live in the city, you know, a banker, a merchant and the secretary of the city board."

John informed him that he was interested in the banker only and wished to visit him as soon as possible.

"I'm sure that he'll receive you now, for I know that he is home," the innkeeper told him. "He never leaves his house at night. I know because he lives just about a block down the street, and his maid is my wife's sister. My son, a lad of fourteen years, will be happy to bring you to his house in the dark." He turned his head and yelled toward the back of the house, "Pierre, Pierre, come here!"

They heard a door slam, another one open and a boy with flaming red hair walked into the room.

"You called me, Father?"

"Bring this Dutch gentleman to Mr. Penetrau, the banker," his father said. "If he wants you to bring him back to the inn, you'll wait for him. If not, you must come home directly."

Although John did not show it, he was pleased. He expected to get a lot of useful information from this boy. He stood up, ready to go.

"I'm Pierre, Sir," the boy said politely. "It's dark outside, but I can fetch a lantern from the stable. It'll make it easier for you to walk, Sir." He opened the door, but took a few steps back. Two men were standing in front of him, wooden sticks in their hands.

"You are the Dutch official, right?" a heavy-set man asked John.

"Yes, I am. My name is John Van het Woudt. You are the sheriff, I suppose? It's good of you to come. I need some information that you may be able to supply. Let's sit down at the table and get better acquainted. Pierre, you see that I can't come with you now. Please, wait for me. I don't think that these gentlemen will stay long," John said.

The sheriff understood properly the hidden menace in John's remark that it was good of him to come. He decided that John couldn't be a common traveler as he had suspected when the innkeeper's servant had reported that a Dutch official had arrived. He winked to his companion to follow John to the table, where John gave him his credentials from the Dutch government. The sheriff read them carefully, surprised that a Dutchman would come to this city. Even Dutch sailors had avoided Dunkerque lately, afraid to be jailed when the expected war started. Abruptly, he asked John why he had come to Dunkerque when his credentials mentioned only his appointment in Paris. John, who had expected this question, explained that he had a special assignment from the Minister of Finance, Seigneur de Pontchartrain. He showed the letter of recommendation, which the sheriff also read carefully. After folding it again he returned it to John, who put it in his breast pocket.

"I understand that I'm to give you all the help necessary for you to accomplish your assignment. What can I do for you, if anything, Mr. Van het Woudt?"

"As you read, I have to interrogate the Huguenots on board the war galleys. Are any galleys in the harbor, and if so, how many?" John asked.

"At this moment only one. It came five days ago. It's name is La Palme. Chevalier de Langeron[23] is its captain. We expect the other one to arrive sometime next week. As a rule, we try to avoid having them both in the harbor at the same time," the sheriff replied.

"Excellent. Where can I find Chevalier de Langeron?"

"He always stays with his cousin, Mr. Gervaise, in the Rue St. Dominique, but in the mornings he is usually on his ship for a short time."

"I'll visit him at his cousin's house or on the galley to arrange for my interrogations of the Huguenot convicts. I need also to see a Mr. Penetrau, a banker," John explained. "I need money and will cash a Letter of Exchange directed to him. Two or three days will take care of my assignments, I think. That is good because Seigneur de Pontchartrain expects me back in Paris as soon as possible."

"Would you like to have one of my men to show you around in town?" the sheriff asked, pleased that John would leave so soon.

"No, I don't think so. Pierre, the son of the innkeeper, is willing to help me." While he was talking, John reflected that it was quite safe to discuss the possibility that the Huguenots were receiving money from the Dutch. After all, the government in Paris and the Lazarists suspected it, and it was most likely that the sheriff had also tried to discover the man who delivered the money to them.

"Your merchants must have a lot of trade with the Dutch, I think," John said conversationally.

"Not anymore," the sheriff said ruefully. "The rumors of war have stopped all trade. You won't see any foreign ships in the harbor nowadays."

---

[23] Chevalier de Langeron was one of the few captains who treated the Huguenot galley slaves as fair as possible, considering the circumstances.

"Well, that takes care of part of my assignment. Seigneur de Pontchartrain would like to know if the Huguenots receive money from the Dutch, and who would be the man to distribute it. Do you have any idea, Sheriff?"

"Nobody knows, not even those from the mission! We've investigated it thoroughly, without success."

"What about your bankers?" John asked casually. "They are used to dealing with Dutch money, I think. Mr. Penetrau is still dealing with them, for his name is on my Letter of Exchange."

Instead of answering the question the sheriff began to laugh. His companion, a constable, could not help smiling, as well.

"I'm sorry, but your question is really amusing. If it was that simple we would have found out long ago. As far as Mr. Penetrau is concerned, he won't deal with the Huguenots. He is a fine member of the Roman Church and hates the Huguenots. Your Letter of Exchange is regular business and has nothing to do with them. All these problems will be solved anyway when the war starts. I think that in less than a few months we will be at each others throats. It'll be impossible to get money from Holland when that happens. You don't think that our king will allow us to trade with our enemies, do you? Mr. Penetrau is known as a reliable trustworthy man, but even he won't dare to do business with your people in the future if war breaks out. It would be even more difficult for any other banker or merchant to get money from the Dutch for the Huguenots. I think that they had better prepare themselves for a time of living on galley rations only. Who knows, maybe it will help to get them converted?"

"Well, thank you," John replied, standing up. "I don't need you anymore, but will keep you up-to-date on my activities in your city. Goodbye, gentlemen." He went to the innkeeper, who was cleaning wine glasses and told him that he had changed his plans and didn't need his son that night.

The sheriff and his constable were dumbfounded that John dismissed them so unexpectedly. However, they did not dare to antagonize a messenger of the king. They left the inn grumbling to each other about the rudeness of the Dutch.

6

THE BISHOP AND THE CHAPLAIN

FATHER Sebastian, the Dominican[24] chaplain, was sitting on his bunk in the tiny room assigned to him aboard the war galley La Palme. He was in low spirits and even felt frightened after his nasty dream. Again, he saw himself running toward the gates of his monastery. The bishop, running behind him, was pulling on his habit in an effort to stop him. A large crowd of Lazarists were following them, yelling and screaming that he was a traitor and heretic and should be hung! His fright gave him incredible power, so much that he could run the long, long way to the monastery without becoming tired. At last he reached the gate, jumped to the large bell, and began sounding it so loudly that it could be heard everywhere. Many more Lazarists heard it and also came rushing down while he, in desperation, kept pulling the bell rope. Suddenly, he saw the face of the gatekeeper looking through the wicket, asking what he wanted. He yelled that the keeper must open the gate to let him in because the Lazarists were going to kill him. But brother gatekeeper just shook his head mournfully, and said in a sepulchral voice that the monastery wasn't open to renegades. Then the Lazarists had reached him and grasped him from behind. He became entangled in a lot of snakelike arms, which he fought like a madman. At that point he awoke with the sweat running down his face.

What was the meaning of this dream, he wondered. Was the devil trying to scare him into abusing the Huguenot convicts, or did the Lord encourage him to join the Huguenot Church

---

[24] A member of the Roman Catholic order of friars, founded in the year 1215 by Dominic.

by showing that he would be kicked out of the monastery and the Roman Church anyway? He didn't know! The dream was obviously caused by his visit to the bishop and the letter from Père La Chaise to his predecessor, which he had received last night. After some hesitation about the legality of opening it, he had read the letter, but wished now that he hadn't. It was really getting too difficult and too dangerous to be a chaplain on a galley. He must do something to avoid all the calamities about which he had dreamed, but he didn't know what.

Slowly, he stood up. It was nearly noon. He had slept for most of the morning after his late arrival at the ship last night. His head ached from worrying. His trouble was that there was nobody to discuss his problems with. The only one who knew how he felt was the Huguenot convict Jean Marteilhe,[25] the secretary and steward of the captain. Thinking of him, he suddenly felt the need for a long talk. Maybe it would help him to forget the dream.

On his way to the captain's cabin, where he knew Jean to be, he nearly stumbled over an empty bucket used for getting water from the sea. Impulsively, he grasped the rope, and threw the bucket overboard. After it was filled with water he hauled it in, and put it on the deck. He knelt down next to it and pushed his head in the water. It was such a good feeling that he repeated it again and again. His hair and beard were drenched, and the water was even running onto his back and chest. He didn't mind, feeling a lot better now. After squeezing the water out of his hair and beard, he dried his face somewhat with the slip of his habit, kicked the bucket over and continued on his way to the cabin.

---

[25] Jean Marteilhe, being a Huguenot, was caught when he tried to flee the persecution in France in the year 1700 when he was sixteen years old. He was condemned to the galleys and suffered there for thirteen years. At the time of this story he was serving on the war galley La Palme. He was wounded seriously when the galley was involved in a sea battle. He recovered, but was not released, as non-Huguenot convicts usually were after being wounded. The captain gave him the privileged position of secretary and steward because he had become unfit to row. Queen Anne of England purchased his liberty. During the years on the galleys he managed to keep a diary, which was published after he had gained his freedom.

Jean, dressed in bright red pants and jacket,[26] was doing his usual morning chores.

"Good morning, Father Sebastian," he said cheerfully. "Glad to see you again. You had a nice trip?"

"No, it was bad, but it could have been worse," Father Sebastian replied morosely, looking out the window to the quay. "I'm not sure that you'll see me here much longer. Either I'll be sent back to the monastery, or I'll volunteer to return. It's getting too dangerous for me to be lenient to your people, and I can't stand to see their suffering. It's getting on my nerves!"

Jean had not given much attention to the chaplain because he was straightening out the captain's bunk, but now he looked up and asked, "What has happened? It would be very bad for us if you left, you know!"

"Well, the bishop summoned me to appear before him in Ypres," the chaplain began to explain.[27] "When I came there, he told me that the Jesuits and Lazarists had complained that I'm favoring the Reformed in this galley and that I left them in quiet security without trying to convert them."

"We thank the Lord every day," Jean interrupted, "that He made you our chaplain after we had suffered so much from the cruel persecution of your Lazarist predecessor." He turned red, embarrassed, and added. "Oh, I'm sorry. I shouldn't have interrupted you. What did you tell the bishop?"

"The truth, of course. 'My lord,' I replied, 'if Your Highness orders me to exhort them, to press them to listen, and to conform to the Roman Church, that is what I do every day, and no one can prove to the contrary. But if you enjoin me to imitate the other chaplains, who cruelly persecute these poor wretches, I shall tomorrow set out for my monastery.' The bishop must be a kind man himself because without any arguing he accepted my views. He said that he was happy with my conduct and encouraged me to continue my duties as chaplain in the same

---

[26] Convicts were forbidden to dress in any color but red.

[27] Some of the clergy of the Roman church abhorred the persecution of the Huguenots. They tried to be as lenient as possible in their attitudes. This particular interview between the chaplain and this bishop occurred in the year 1706.

way. The next day I heard by the grapevine that he had summoned the other chaplains, and intended to censure them for their methods of conversion.”

“I don’t understand you,” Jean said surprised. “Isn’t it something to thank the Lord for, having received the approval of the bishop?”

“It sounds that way, undoubtedly,” the chaplain agreed, ruefully, “but you don’t know the power of the Lazarists. It has happened before and it will happen again that they find ways and means to get what they want. I wouldn’t even be surprised if they’ll succeed in having the bishop removed.”

“There is time enough to worry about that when it happens,” Jean said cheerfully, but the chaplain didn’t even hear him. He saw the captain coming down the quay, accompanied by a young man, neatly dressed in dark clothing carrying a small valise.

“The captain is coming,” he warned his young friend. “He has somebody with him.” Jean also looked out the window, astonished to see the captain.

“Isn’t that something!” he exclaimed. “In all the years that I have known him he never came to the ship in the afternoon when we are in the harbor.”

“It must have to do with the letter that came yesterday,” the chaplain muttered softly.

Jean heard his muttering, but did not have the time to ask what he meant because the door was opened and both men entered.

“I’m happy to see you again, Father Sebastian,” Chevalier de Langeron said in a good humor. “I hope you had a good trip. Let me introduce you to Mr. John Van het Woudt, a Dutch envoy with a special assignment from our king.”

“Nice to meet you, Mr. Van het Woudt,” the chaplain responded politely.

“Mr. Van het Woudt, this is Father Sebastian, the chaplain of La Palme. The man dressed in red is a Huguenot convict that I use as secretary, steward, and sometimes even as purveyor. He has a privileged position aboard this ship because he is the only Huguenot convict who survived a serious wound in battle. Nevertheless, he wasn't freed, as is the legal right of wounded convicts, because this right doesn't apply to Huguenots."

"I'm delighted to meet you both," John said cheerfully to the chaplain. "It seems to me that you can be a great help in my assignment."

"I have to leave now, Mr. Van het Woudt," Chevalier de Langeron interrupted, "but I'm convinced that Father Sebastian can arrange any interview you desire to conduct. If you have any questions or want to see me again, please, don't hesitate to call on me. Goodbye, Mr. Van het Woudt." He shook hands with them and disappeared.

"Let's sit down," the chaplain suggested. He pulled two chairs close to the table, seated himself, and waited for John, who placed the valise on the table before he sat down.

"My assignment is to have confidential talks with Huguenot convicts to find out if they are acquainted with cloth working and if they know any Huguenots who are skilled workers in this industry. My interviews will be confidential so that I can win their trust and cooperation. I'm aware that it sounds like a strange assignment, but I've a strong recommendation from the government in Paris. Please read it," John said, handing over the recommendation of Seigneur de Pontchartrain. The chaplain took it and read it carefully. He returned it to John without comment, and asked him what he wished.

"It is quite simple. I want to interrogate at least five Huguenot convicts today, confidentially, without any witnesses."

"I'm sorry," Father Sebastian replied, resolutely. "It can't be done. I give you permission to interrogate all Huguenot convicts, but only if I'm there. I don't want secret meetings aboard this ship."

"But, Father Sebastian," John protested, "my recommendation states clearly that you have to give me any help possible. You aren't allowed to obstruct me."

"Mr. Van het Woudt," the chaplain retorted while he shrugged his shoulders contemptuously, "I report to the abbot of my monastery and to the bishop in Ypres. Your request is contrary to my assignment: the spiritual welfare of all the convicts, and the conversion of the Huguenot convicts. If you don't agree with my presence during your interrogations, you better return to Paris for different instructions."

John had never considered the possibility that the chaplain might refuse to follow the recommendation of the Minister of Finance. He tried to convince the chaplain of the importance of his mission, but the chaplain did not give in.

It was a hopeless situation for John, and he ran out of arguments in the discussion. At last, he decided to try a different approach without endangering the Huguenot convicts or himself.

"All right, I'll accept your presence, Father Sebastian," he announced. "Let's begin to interrogate the steward who is here. You have no objections?"

After Father Sebastian had nodded his approval, he turned to Jean Marteilhe who had kept himself in the background, cleaning the cabin.

"Please join us and sit down, Jean. I'd like to talk with you, but I have to warn you first." He watched Father Sebastian when he continued smoothly, "Recently Father Sebastian received a secret missive from Père la Chaise, the father confessor of your king." He saw the chaplain's eyes open wide in surprise.

"In that letter Père La Chaise instructs your chaplain to listen in secret on our conversation, hoping to discover if the Dutch government supports the Huguenot galley slaves with money. He has also been told to find out which banker and Huguenot are the middlemen for the distribution of the money. In addition, they hope that your chaplain may hear the names of Huguenots who are in hiding in France so that they can be caught." Father Sebastian had become more and more anxious, and now he could not control himself.

"How do you know, Mr. Van het Woudt?" He exclaimed. "It was a secret letter sent by a special messenger!"

"Well, I'm glad that you confirm to have received the letter," John replied calmly. "How do I know its contents? That is my secret. In fact, after my visit in Dunkerque I'm supposed to return to Paris and report to Seigneur de Pontchartrain. It's possible that I'll read your report there." Next, he addressed himself to Jean again.

"As you must understand, Jean, it is very important not to say anything that can be used by the Jesuits to make the persecution more severe."

"You are mistaken, Sir," said Jean, who had quietly listened to the discussion, with a smile on his face. "I have known Father Sebastian for a long time. He is an honorable man, and will not report anything that will increase our suffering. He has proven more than once to have pity on us. Father Sebastian and the captain can't liberate us, but they try their utmost to reduce our suffering as much as possible." John looked doubtfully from Jean to the chaplain wondering what to do. Could he trust a priest with the confidential information of the Huguenots?

"How do I know that Father Sebastian or you, for that matter, won't betray them?" he asked dubiously.

"How do we know that you can be trusted?" Jean retorted. "As far as we are concerned, you could be a traitor, trying to get information from us. We trust you only because you are from Holland. As far as Father Sebastian is concerned, I can prove to you that he can be trusted, provided that you are indeed a special envoy from the Dutch government."

After John had assured them that it was true and that he had come with a special mission, Jean turned to the chaplain and suggested that they would report his dealings with the banker. Father Sebastian assented, glad that Jean was willing to defend him.

7

THE CHAPLAIN AND THE BANKER

"FATHER Sebastian had a tough problem with the banker who received money for us from Holland. I want to explain how we, Huguenots, got an excellent relationship with the chaplain before I talk about the difficulties with the banker," Jean began.[28]

"Three years ago, our chaplain, a Lazarist who used his powers to abuse us badly, died. Chevalier de Langeron, our captain, didn't want to wait long for a replacement and engaged Father Sebastian, a monk of the Dominican order. At first, he treated us as badly as he could, but in time he relented and conformed to our captain's lenient way of acting. The ill treatment that we had endured was succeeded by obliging acts toward us all and especially to me, being the captain's steward. During the last few years, scarcely a day passes in which we don't have a chat. He is a learned man, and as I often receive religious books[29] from Holland, he asked me one day if I had some sermons to lend him. Though his request appeared suspicious to me, I offered him a volume of sermons, which he punctually returned. It was so much to his taste that I then lent him all my books, all of which he returned to me.

---

[28] The historical events told in this, and the previous chapter (the interview with the bishop and the traitorous effort of Mr. Penetrau), were recorded in the diary of Jean Marteilhe after he gained his freedom.

[29] Huguenots were not allowed to have any books. They were smuggled aboard in the same way as money and other gifts. In this particular case, a Turk called Aly, a purchased slave who was allowed to go ashore when the ship was in the harbor (Huguenots were never allowed to leave the ship), served as the go-between person. Regularly, the Lazarists made unexpected searches for the books and other forbidden material. The captain of La Palme, in support of the Huguenots, always warned them one day prior to the search so that they could hide the books and other gifts, often aided by the other convicts who were not searched.

"One day, in a conversation he asked me if we, members of the Reformed Church, didn't receive money from Holland. I thought it best to reply negatively on this subject, for fear of the consequences.

"Initially, we received our money from Holland by means of a banker named Mr. Piecourt. However, he went bankrupt, and our remittances were entrusted to another banker, Mr. Penetrau." Here John listened very attentively. This was the banker who had become suspicious to Mr. De Groot.

"Mr. Penetrau had paid me three times at regular intervals, but then he experienced some financial problems. He tried to solve them by ruining me. He received an order from Amsterdam to pay me one hundred crowns.[30] He wanted the money himself and needed a plausible reason for keeping it without alarming his Amsterdam correspondent about his financial problems. He went to our chaplain, Father Sebastian, fully aware that he was about to sacrifice me so that he might maintain his credit. He declared in strict confidence that he had an order from Holland to pay me one hundred crowns, but that he wished first to ask the chaplain's permission because the prohibition of the court made him afraid to meddle in such affairs. Mr. Penetrau thought that the chaplain, far from granting it, would at once forbid it. In that case, he expected to keep the money and to be out of his financial difficulties. He didn't care that I would have been exposed to an examination, which would not have taken place without a furious bastinado to make me confess which bankers had paid me the money before."

Here Father Sebastian interrupted the story, his voice quavering with anger.

"I understood what the consequences of this affair might be, and looking directly at Mr. Penetrau, I said to him, 'I'm sure, Sir, this isn't the first time that you've made similar payments without asking permission. Your correspondents in Holland are not so imprudent as to entrust you with such a commission without being certain by experience that you'll perform it. However,

---

³⁰ 100 Crowns = 25 Louis d'Ors = approximately the wages for 1½ years for a skilled laborer.

as it seems to depend on my permission, I willingly grant it.'
Mr. Penetrau was much disconcerted by this reply, which he
hadn't expected. The scoundrel told me that my permission
would not secure him from danger, and that he would see the
master of the galleys and ask him for permission. I was annoyed
at this reply and said sharply, 'What, Sir? After you've given
me to understand that my consent would decide you, you dare
to tell me that you'll apply to the master? You can do as you
please. But, remember that if you mention a word of it to the
master or to anyone else, I have a very long arm, and I know
how to reach you and make you repent of it.'

"Penetrau, utterly vanquished and not knowing what to do,
confessed that he was a little short of cash, and that although
one hundred crowns wouldn't bring him to extremities, he didn't
possess them at the moment. He said that if Jean would wait a
fortnight and not write to Holland to say that he hadn't received
this sum, he would pay him without failure at the end of that
time. I told him that he had done well to confess the matter to
me, and that I would forgive his previous transgressions. 'But,'
I said, 'I'll not run the risk of being your dupe. To ensure your
punctuality, make me out a note for the one hundred crowns,
payable in fifteen days, which I'll remit to the person to whom
you have to pay it, and I'll procure you a receipt. You can make
yourself quite easy about Marteilhe. I'll pledge you my word
that he'll not write to Amsterdam before the bill is due.' Penetrau,
quite pleased that the matter had taken this turn, readily drew
up the note."

"That same day, Father Sebastian came to the galley," Jean
continued. "He called me into the stern-cabin, and at once said
to me, with a serious air, 'I'm surprised that a confessor of the
truth dares to lie to a man of my character.' I was taken quite
aback by this speech, and told him that I didn't know what he
meant.

" 'Haven't you told me,' he said, 'that you don't receive
money from Holland, nor from any other place? I hold in my
hand that which convicts you of this falsehood,' and he showed
me the note Mr. Penetrau had made out for him.

" 'Do you know what this is?' he asked.

" 'Yes, Sir,' I replied. 'I see that it's some money that belongs to you.'

" 'It doesn't belong to me,' said Father Sebastian, 'but to you.' And then he related all that had passed between Penetrau and himself, and giving me the letter of advice, he again reproached me for having lied. I took the liberty to tell him that he was no less guilty than I was, for, knowing that it was not a thing that I could confess, he had obliged me to deny it by asking me. He agreed to this, and told me that in a fortnight he would bring me the one hundred crowns. This he did punctually to the day, and while counting them out, he offered me his services.

" 'Write to your friends in Holland,' he said, 'that they can address their remittances to me, and be assured that I'll pay them promptly to you and you'll avoid all risks.' I thanked him for his kindness, but I didn't think I ought to make use of it.

"I hope I've convinced you, Mr. Van het Woudt, that our chaplain can be trusted."

"Yes," John admitted. "Your story is quite convincing. However, I don't understand why you, Father Sebastian, didn't directly explain to me your convictions. It would have made everything much simpler."

"I didn't know you, either," the chaplain explained. "I needed some time to study you and to make up my mind. I think that we can trust each other, and I promise that I won't write anything in my report to Père La Chaise that could hinder you. Let's now return to our business. I must stay with you when you are talking with the Huguenot convicts, though."

"I can't say how pleased I am that everything has been cleared up," John said. "I was afraid that I couldn't do my assignments, which would be disastrous for the Huguenot convicts and would defeat my personal goal. It's no use to go into details, but I can tell you at least enough to understand my reasons for this visit."

8

JOHN EXPLAINS HIS ASSIGNMENTS

"FIRST I want to explain that I haven't one assignment, but three," John said, beginning the account of the reason for his visit to the galleys. "One assignment from Seigneur de Pontchartrain, one from the Dutch government, and one from myself.

"Jean, the first assignment is for you and all other Huguenot convicts. The Minister of Finance feels that the economy of France will improve a lot if the Huguenots could be persuaded to return to their jobs. He feels that France is hard hit by the loss of the clothing industry. It's well known that Huguenots are needed to work in this industry, even if enough Dutch people would come over to help. Therefore, he suggested that I talk with Huguenots and try to discover which ones are capable workers in this trade. The Minister will offer them certain privileges so that the industry can be started up again."

The chaplain and Jean listened, but both their expressions revealed that they were skeptical of this offer.

"Will we have freedom of religion? Will we be allowed to go to the Reformed church again? Will the children be restored to their parents?[31]" Jean asked.

"I don't think so," John replied, shaking his head. "Therefore, I would never accept that offer, however good it sounds. I'm convinced that any Huguenot who agrees, will be forced to deny Christ and eventually be worse off than he is now. Don't forget, this is my official assignment. However, the secret goal of your government is well expressed in the letter that you,

---

[31] Most children younger than sixteen years were taken away from Huguenot parents and brought to monasteries and convents, where they were brought up as members of the Roman church.

Father Sebastian, received yesterday — to find the names of the men who are willing to risk their life in being the middlemen between the Dutch and the Huguenot convicts. Nevertheless, my official assignment is an excellent cover for me to do my other duties.

"Another of my assignments is to give twenty Louis d'Ors to the Huguenots on the galleys," John continued. "I intended to give them to Mr. Penetrau, but now that I've heard of your difficulties with him, I won't do that. I can't give them to Jean either because then Father Sebastian must report his name to Père La Chaise. I think that the best solution is to give the money to you, Father Sebastian. You know how to take care of it, I trust. The advantage is that you can report truthfully that I have not given any money to any Huguenots."

Hearing John's suggestion, the chaplain began to laugh. John and Jean joined him, not so much because they thought John's proposal so hilarious, but rather because the chaplain's laughter was so catching. At last the chaplain stopped laughing.

"Well, I haven't heard such a good joke in ages, a Dominican monk receiving Dutch money to help French heretics," Father Sebastian said, still smiling. "Now, tell me your third assignment. Are you going to ask the Pope to become Reformed?" he joked.

"Dunkerque is hardly the place where I can ask the Pope such questions," John responded, smiling.

"This assignment is more personal. My father is also a Huguenot, convicted for life on one of the war galleys. Nobody has heard from him and I'm wondering if you know where he may be. His name is John Dubois," John responded, confident that Father Sebastian wouldn't betray him.

"Aha," exclaimed the chaplain. "You aren't Dutch at all, and your name isn't Van het Woudt. I was wondering all the time because I felt that you speak French too well, without any accent at all. Do you really have these assignments or are they also faked ones? Oh, no, your letter of recommendation is true enough, I think. Now you had better explain everything."

"Yes, I am a Huguenot, but a few years ago I fled with my little sister to Holland. I work in an office in Amsterdam, as the secretary of an important banker, and that is how I got these assignments," John explained simply. "What do you think? Have you heard from my father?"

Father Sebastian and Jean Marteilhe looked at each other, trying to recall anybody with the name Dubois. They shook their heads.

"I never heard about such a person," Jean said, and the chaplain agreed.

"Are you sure that he hasn't adopted another name?" Jean asked. "That happens sometimes."

"What does he look like?" the chaplain added.

"Well, he is tall and muscular. Black hair, his nose slightly bowed. His eyes are pitch black. He was a forester and had two children, myself and my sister Manette. Wait, he had a scar on his left hand where he was once bitten by a dog," John summed up.

"Oh, that must be John l'Ardeur,"[32] both exclaimed.

"He got his name because he had lots of mettle and was an example for everybody in testifying about his faith," Jean explained. "He sat next to me on the rowers' bench for more than two years. Sometimes he talked about his children, and I think he mentioned your name and also your sister's name. I'm sure that he must be your father. Don't you think that John resembles him, Father Sebastian?"

"Yes, very much so," the chaplain agreed, looking at John. "I never thought of your relationship, but now I see that you look like a young version of your father. I agree with Jean that John l'Ardeur must be your father."

"You sat next to him? So he must be on this galley," John said eagerly. "Can I see him, or do I have to ask for special permission? What are the rules here?"

Both shook their heads and Father Sebastian said, "He isn't on this galley anymore. Two weeks ago we were in La Rochelle, and were told to leave most of the Huguenot convicts there. He belonged to that group. We don't know why he had to stay

---

³² L'ardeur means the one who is burning with eagerness.

because most of them were too sick to row while he was in excellent condition. It's most likely that they will be transferred to another galley with a lack of convicts. That happens every once in awhile.

"Don't be discouraged, though, Mr. Van het Woudt. Maybe his transfer is advantageous for you. We left La Rochelle three weeks ago, but a transfer always takes a very long time. I doubt that this group has been assigned to another ship yet. It may take many more weeks. That's good for you, if you are going to La Rochelle. It's entirely possible that he is still ashore, which will make it much easier to find him."

It was a disappointment for John to hear that his father had left this galley only three weeks ago. However, it was a large step forward to knowing where he was. That would make it much easier to contact him. All things considered, he was fortunate to get this information during his first visit to the galleys. The Lord was actually helping him in everything he had to do, he thought with a thankful heart.

Under these circumstances, he would, of course, go to La Rochelle. It would become more dangerous when they found out in Paris that he didn't return. It was even more so now that war had been declared. He must figure out a way to avoid getting spies after him. As far as home was concerned, he could take his time. The Dutch ambassador and Mr. De Groot had promised to give the message to Manette that it might take several months before she would see him again in Amsterdam.

All at once he perceived that the chaplain and Jean had been waiting for him to say something while he was considering how to proceed.

"Father Sebastian," he addressed the chaplain, "This afternoon I have not only learned to trust you, but also to value your opinion. I'm supposed to return to Paris after I've interrogated the Huguenots on this ship. I'll go, of course, to La Rochelle, as you'll understand. I don't think that it's necessary to interrogate more Huguenots. They might believe in the offer of Seigneur de Pontchartrain, expecting to get the freedom to serve the Lord properly. I can't explain the secret purpose of your government in this proposal without endangering my own position. The less people know about my disguise, the safer it is. Therefore, I'll not talk with them, but leave in one or two days, depending on how fast I can conclude my other assignment, and how well I can hide my tracks. I trust that you don't have to mention to anyone where I'm going, Father Sebastian?" The chaplain assured him that he didn't see a need for revealing what he knew about John to anybody.

"Two more matters must be resolved before I can leave Dunkerque. I have been requested by my master to find out more about Mr. Penetrau. You have told me well enough that he can't be trusted, but you can keep him under control, right?" After the chaplain and Jean had stated that they agreed, he mentioned that in that case he needn't worry about finding another banker. He'd have a talk with Mr. Penetrau anyway.

"The other assignment I mentioned before. I have the pleasure of bringing twenty Louis d'Ors to help the suffering Huguenots on the galleys. This is a special gift from the late King William of Orange, the Dutch Republic, and the Huguenot Churches of Amsterdam." While he was talking, he unclasped his valise, which was still standing on the table, and took out a tiny box. He opened it so that the others couldn't see its contents, and took out enough golden coins to lay four rows of five coins on the table.

"Here they are," he said smiling. "You don't have to give me a receipt, Father Sebastian. Just give them to the proper people, that's all."

"Thanks a lot, Mr. Van het Woudt," Father Sebastian laughed, and moved the rows to Jean. "You receive this money from me, as you see. It is a present from King William of Orange, the Dutch Republic, and the French Huguenot Churches in Amsterdam. Please, remember that I gave them to you, and nobody else. Mr. Van het Woudt can testify that no banker or Huguenot acted as the middleman." And he laughed again, loud.

"I don't know if you have received the news that the Dutch Republic and its allies have formally declared war on France," John mentioned after the laughter had died down. The astonished faces of Father Sebastian and Jean showed him that they hadn't heard the news.

"That creates a problem," John added. "How can the Dutch government continue its practice of giving money to the suffering Huguenots during war time?" All three of them frowned and concentrated on finding a solution to this problem. At last, they had to admit to each other that they didn't know how to keep in contact.

"I suggest that the monies be delivered to me," Father Sebastian said thoughtfully. "That's safer. I don't know who can deliver it to me. Maybe the Dutch can find a French fisherman who is willing to cooperate. If they receive the money in the open sea, they could bring it to me."

John and Jean agreed that it was a possible solution and John promised to suggest it in Amsterdam.

"I have one more request, but I don't know if it can be done," John said, wavering somewhat. "Chevalier de Langeron brought me aboard without giving me an opportunity to see the convicts. The only thing I noticed was the crowded deck with, as far as I know, soldiers. I assume that the convicts have to remain below deck. I'd like to see their quarters, if possible. Can you guide me along, Father Sebastian?"

The chaplain looked seriously at John, then turned his eyes down toward his hands and replied as a man completely embarrassed, "John, I would like to show you all around, and if you insist upon it, I will do it. Nevertheless, I strongly advise against it, for a very good reason. The space below decks where the convicts stay is so vermin-infected that you'll see the convicts covered with lice and fleas. If you desire to go there, I'll suggest that you put on a nightgown, which you can strip off when you leave, so that you can rid yourself of most of the vermin. I do the same myself when I have to go there. You can't get rid of all the vermin that way, though. I suggest that instead of going below deck, Jean can tell you more about the conditions there."

John had listened with abhorrence to the chaplain's words.

"Yes, I'm afraid you are right, Father Sebastian. Jean, I understand that you have lived there several years before you became secretary of the captain. Please, give me some idea how the conditions are, so that I can report it to the Dutch government."

"The conditions below deck are horrible,"[33] Jean began talking slowly. But gradually he began to speak faster as if he desired to finish the account of the terrible situation as fast as possible.

"There are five convicts to every oar. A Turk, purchased by the government, is seated at the end of the oar on the highest part of the bench. The seats of the five convicts are gradually lower so that the one at the lower end of the oar sits the lowest. The Turks are strong. When the ship is in the harbor, they are allowed to go ashore alone any time they want. The other convicts are also allowed ashore provided they wear their chains and are accompanied by their under officer. It costs money because they have to pay him. The Huguenots are never allowed ashore. However, the Turk slaves are very willing to help them. For example, one particular Turk always picks up the money at the banker and brings it to me for distribution among the Huguenots.

"Rowing is very strenuous work. The convicts must rise to draw their stroke, and fall back again almost on their backs, so that in every season the sweat trickles from their backs. If they show any weakness or are not keeping the exact rhythm, they and their neighbors are unmercifully beaten with a tough wand. To make the punishment harsh, the convicts are not allowed to cover their upper body while rowing. The food is adequate, but bad tasting."

"I don't want to talk about it anymore," Jean ended. "Life there is too horrible. Yet, many strong men survive a long time. The other ones get sick and are left in a dirty, dark cubicle to die."

John had listened quietly, horrified by the picture Jean was describing. At last he stood up.

"My friends, I have to leave. I'm sorry that I can't do more than just bring you money, but I'll certainly report the conditions

---

[33] The following description of the life aboard the war galleys, and the treatment of the convicts are historical facts. The treatment was far worse than the impression of this description.

of the poor Huguenot slaves. I hope, Jean, that the Lord will bless you and strengthen your faith in Him, who is also our Comforter here. Goodbye."

He shook hands with Jean and with Father Sebastian, who silently guided him across the deck to the quay.

"Father Sebastian, thank you for the support you give these poor wretches. I hope that you will also be guided so that you will acknowledge that the Lord desires to be served only in accordance with his own Word. I'll pray for you. Goodbye."

Father Sebastian shook his hand and said, "Goodbye, John. May the Lord bless you."

*   *   *

That evening, John and Pierre visited Mr. Penetrau, the banker. John gave him the Letter of Exchange and received the forty Louis d'Ors. In the ensuing conversation, he asked for specific directions concerning the shortest route to the Spanish Netherlands in the North. After a friendly exchange, they left and went to the sheriff. He told the sheriff that he had accomplished his assignments and would be on his way the next morning when the city gates were open. He left with a cool goodbye.

Early the next morning during breakfast John invited the innkeeper to sit down at his table. He explained that he had completed his assignment and would leave presently. He left a good tip for Pierre and, at his request, the innkeeper explained the road north to the Spanish Netherlands. It was completely safe to travel, he added, understanding that John intended to go there on his way to the Dutch Republic.

After a cordial goodbye John left, his papers in his breast pocket and his valise attached to his saddle. The horse was well fed and rested so that the trip to La Rochelle promised to be an easy one. He was amused, hoping that his trick would be successful. The innkeeper and Mr. Penetrau were thinking that he was traveling north to the Spanish Netherlands although he was actually going to the south. Maybe they wouldn't find him if they were going to look for him, he hoped.

9

THE SISTERS RABOTEAU[34]

THE girl rode her beautiful, well-groomed horse along a narrow lane toward the mansion, an imposing three-story building which dominated the wooded park-like area. A groom followed her on a large stallion at a distance of three or four horse lengths. In front of the main entrance she dismounted easily and gave the reins to the servant. She turned again to her horse, petted its neck lightly, and addressed the man in a friendly but somewhat commanding tone.

"Hercule, Belle deserves a good rubbing down after her exercise. Make sure that she's properly curried, too," she added, and then darted up the stairs to the door of the mansion, which was opened by a footman, who had apparently seen her coming. In the hall, a woman servant carrying a basket moved aside and made a curtsy.

"Where is Madeleine?" the girl asked.

"Miss Madeleine is in her bedroom. She wants to be left alone. She doesn't feel well, Miss Jaqueline."

Jaqueline frowned, and walking much slower now, she ascended the wide stairs to the next floor. She had gone horse riding alone today because her sister Madeleine, who had beautiful handwriting, had been called by their uncle to write a letter for him. Something unusual must have happened, she decided, knowing that Madeleine often had a headache when she was upset.

She opened the door of their bedroom and walked inside, closing the door carefully behind her. It was a large room furnished with two beds against one wall and a small table with two chairs

---

[34] The story of the sisters Raboteau actually happened during those times.

close to an open window, which let in the fragrant smell of the trees.

On one of the beds, a girl was lying with her head on her arms, crying bitterly. Jaqueline threw her hat and riding quirt on the floor and hurried to the crying girl. She fell on her knees next to the bed and put her hand on her sister's head.

"What has happened, Madeleine? Why are you crying? Did someone hurt you?"

Madeleine turned to her and tried unsuccessfully to stop sobbing.

"Oh, dear. Please try to control yourself. Tell your little sister what is bothering you. Everything will be fine. Come on, don't lie down. Sit up," Jaqueline said, and grasped her sister's arm, forcing her to sit against the headboard of the bed.

"That's better. Now just wait while I get some water so that you can wash your face. Your nose is as red as a beet. Don't move now. I'll be back soon."

Presently, she returned with a cloth soaked in cold water.

"Can you wash your face yourself or shall I do it?"

Without waiting for a reply she washed her sister's face and smoothed her hair.

"Well, that feels better, doesn't it? Now tell me what is going on. I never expected you to be so upset after your letter writing. Was Uncle Claude really so bad?"

Sitting close together on the bed, it was easy to see the two were sisters, although they did not look that much alike. Jaqueline, the younger of the two at sixteen years old, was a lively girl with a very dark complexion. Madeleine, a lighter colored brunette was one year older than her sister and was by far more quiet. She had now recovered enough to talk with only an occasional sob.

"Uncle Claude was alone when I came into the library," she told Jaqueline. "He gave me a piece of paper on which he had written some notes. I had to put it in proper letter form, as I have done so often for him. It was addressed to the Comte[35]

---

[35] Comte = Count.

de Montfort. I didn't like it because Uncle Claude and Aunt Isabeau tell me all the time that I should marry his son. The letter was quite simple, though. It was only an invitation for the Comte and his family to come to Uncle Claude's party in Paris on September 6. I wrote the letter while Uncle Claude waited. When it was ready, he stood up and abruptly told me . . ." Madeleine broke off, began to sob again vehemently, but soon recovered enough to continue her story. She told her sister that their uncle had said he had made up his mind. He would send her to the Convent of the Ursulines[36] unless she would agree on the day before the party to become a New Convert[37] and to marry the young Vicomte[38] de Montfort in Paris at the party.

"He said that joining the Roman Church had saved his neck and fortune five years ago and that he didn't intend to risk losing it just because two stubborn, silly girls didn't know what was good for them. It was a decent choice, he pointed out, because we have no other relatives than him and are not allowed to leave the country. You also will have to make the same choice on the same day, he said. He even tried to be nice by suggesting that he would be willing to look for other husbands, provided they were Roman Catholic.

"Oh, Jacqueline, I am so scared. I don't want to become a New Convert. We cannot partake in killing the Lord Jesus every day in the Mass.[39] However, I don't want to be jailed for life in a convent, either. What can we do? Why doesn't the Lord help us? We pray every day for our delivery and nothing happens. We don't even know if our Church still exists. We haven't seen any other Huguenot after Dad and Mom died last year and we

---

[36] The Ursulines, an order of nuns with very strict rules, were well known for the teaching of young girls.

[37] Huguenots who rejoined the Roman church were commonly called "New Converts."

[38] Vicomte = Viscount.

[39] The Huguenots abhorred the celebration and partaking of the Mass more than anything else. They understood that the priest, who administers the Mass, sacrifices Jesus Christ again, which they considered to be a cursed idolatry as expressed in the Heidelberg Catechism. In the sermons and literature of that time they referred frequently to a text from Paul's Letter to the Corinthians: one cannot drink the cup of the Lord and the cup of demons (1 Cor. 10:21).

came to live with Uncle Claude and Aunt Isabeau. Maybe the Lord has forgotten about us."

Jaqueline put her hand on her sister's mouth and said sternly, "Hush, Madeleine. You don't know what you are saying. Don't sin by even thinking such evil thoughts. Of course the Lord takes care of us. We know it for sure. Don't you dare to doubt it! He is guiding us, even if we have to go to that Convent. We aren't there yet, though. We've still got four weeks, and who knows? Maybe we'll find a way to escape. Let's not talk about it now. You know what we'll do? I'll get something for supper and tell them that we are going to bed early. After supper, we'll have our devotion time, and we'll ask the Lord especially to help us to trust Him and for a means to escape the Convent.

*   *   *

"I never expected to sleep as well as I did," Madeleine remarked the next morning. "I slept all my worries away and feel as good as new. I'm ashamed that I got so upset last night. After all, you were right. Even in a Convent, we belong to Jesus Christ."

"I'm glad you are your old self again," said Jaqueline cheerfully. "I didn't sleep that well, though, because I've been planning for escape. You agree that we should try to run away, right?"

"Of course, but we can't talk about it now for they need us downstairs. Let's go over your plans this afternoon."

Both girls ran downstairs to do their morning chores. Aunt Isabeau had given them a tight daily schedule like most girls of their class. They had to rise early and were taught in the morning how to direct the servants and do regular household duties. After lunch they were allowed to go horse riding and late in the afternoon they went to their room to sew or do embroidery. The girls liked that time of the day best because their busy fingers never stopped them from chattering or having fun, without being overheard.

Uncle Claude and Aunt Isabeau treated their nieces well enough, but they made sure that they could not run away. That would anger the parochial priest and could have unpleasant consequences. Therefore, the girls were guarded well but unobtrusively. They were allowed to go horse riding, but a groom always went with them. Even when they went for a walk, they were accompanied by one of the maidservants.

It was quite common for Jaqueline to begin talking when they were sitting at the window in their room. She had an active imagination, brimming over with stories, jokes, and plans. Madeleine hated to make plans or decisions and usually let herself be guided by her younger sister. She was the one who discovered if Jaqueline's plans would not work, though, and Jaqueline knew she was usually right.

"Running away sounds so easy but it's more difficult than I first thought," Jaqueline began that afternoon. "It's rather obvious that we must go to England. To do that we must find a skipper who is willing to hide us in his boat, but we'll never find one staying here with Uncle Claude and Aunt Isabeau. We must leave here and stay in La Rochelle without them being able to find us. Honestly, I haven't the faintest idea how to do it. Leaving the mansion without being discovered is difficult enough, but hiding in La Rochelle is even worse. Running away in the daytime? Forget about it. We would be caught in no time. Going by night is also dangerous unless we have someone to guide and protect us. Where can we find a trustworthy person? Really, I don't know what to do!"

"Well, well, it doesn't happen often that you throw up your hands for lack of ideas," Madeleine said teasingly. "You seem to have forgotten our advantage. The Lord God Himself is on our side. We have His promise that He will take care of us, whatever happens.

"You didn't even mention our biggest problem: money. Don't worry about it, though, because I solved it already. I've got the diamond ring and earbobs I inherited from our Mother. We both have other jewelry, which can also be sold. I think that it will be more than enough to go to England. Once there, we can get all kinds of help from other Huguenots.

"We don't have to look for a skipper, either. You must have forgotten our uncle, Jean Charles, who went years ago to England.

I'm not sure but I think he lives now in Dublin, an important harbor of Ireland. Every year he comes a few times to La Rochelle where he buys wine and fruit. He fled France because he is a Huguenot and will certainly help us if he hears of our difficulties. However, I don't know when he comes to France, nor how to get in touch with him. Maybe we've got to hide with someone in La Rochelle, as you suggested, but who?"

Jaqueline looked up from her needlework to ask, "Do you know if our old nurse is still alive, Madeleine? She was always so nice. What happened to her after she left our house?"

"I don't know where she lives exactly," Madeleine answered. "She went to La Rochelle, but being a Huguenot it was difficult for her to get another job as a children's nurse. When her husband passed away she had no other choice than to become a washerwoman."

"What do you think? Would she be willing to help?"

"Oh, she would! Certainly!" Madeleine replied. "She'll do anything for us. She really loved us, but we can't ask her. Even if we were able to send her a message, I doubt that she could do a thing. It would be far too dangerous, and I don't think that she can afford it."

"Oh, but hiding us isn't dangerous. If she lives alone, nobody needs to find out. I think our biggest problem is to locate her," Jaqueline remarked. "I'm wondering if we have a maidservant who would be willing to look for her if we give her a set of earbobs."

"I don't like that idea at all. She may betray us when she can get more money." Madeleine argued, "I wouldn't be surprised if running away, dressed up as a pair of peasant girls, isn't a better solution. At least we wouldn't attract attention. We've still more than three weeks before Uncle Claude's party. Let's wait as long as possible until we are certain that we'll succeed. We may get better ideas, who knows?"

Jaqueline agreed, but decided that she would try to find out which servant could be used best for running messages.

10

THE FOREIGN VISITOR

"WHO is that fellow coming to the house?" Jaqueline wondered aloud. "Look, his horse is lame in the left hind quarter."

It was late in the afternoon, several days after the sisters had made up their mind to run away to England, and both were sitting at the table in their room. Tired of her embroidery work, Jaqueline was looking out the window.

The young man approaching the mansion was neatly but soberly dressed. He walked at the head of his horse with his arm through the reins and led him to the bottom of the wide stairs leading to the ornamental oak front door. There he carelessly threw the reins over one of the posts of the handrail, and unbuckled a valise that was attached behind the saddle. He took it in his hand and went up the stairs to the door. A groom soon came and took the horse away in the direction of the stables.

The girls had watched the unusual event with great interest. Jaqueline had given most of her attention to the horse while Madeleine had scrutinized the young man whom they both agreed was very good-looking.

Half an hour later, a maidservant knocked on the door. Having received permission to enter, she brought a message that Madame Raboteau, their aunt, requested them to wear their best dresses for supper because an unexpected visitor had arrived. Supper would be served half an hour later than usual. They asked the maid eagerly who the visitor was, but she only knew that he had come from another country, from Holland.

Excited about the unexpected news the girls jumped up to make themselves ready. It was a nice break in their monotonous daily routine, especially since the young man was so handsome.

Downstairs, Madame herself was supervising the preparation of the supper table, which was being laid ready by a few servants.

In the meantime, the visitor was sitting with his host in the library, drinking a good glass of wine. He had introduced himself as John Van het Woudt, and had explained that he came from Holland for some government business in La Rochelle. His horse had lost one of his shoes and had begun to stumble when he was close to Pont-Gibaud. A farmer working in the field had suggested that he could get help at the mansion.

John apologized for the trouble he was causing, and showed his host the letter of recommendation from Seigneur de Pontchartrain, Minister of Finance of King Louis XIV. After reading it, Mr. Raboteau felt that John, who was on a mission supported by the French government, was important enough to join the family for supper. John thanked him profusely for his hospitality, and asked if a blacksmith was available to look after his horse. His host informed him that the smith lived in another village, but that he would arrange for a stable boy to bring the horse to the smith early the next morning.

"It's an unhappy circumstance for you that you must stay overnight," he added politely, "but fortunate for us to have such a pleasant guest under our roof."

Initially, John felt ill at ease at the supper table especially when the girls joined them. As the secretary of Mr. De Groot, he was used to simple meals and simple living quarters. Now he was sitting at a fashionable supper table in the house of a noble, and in the company of ladies. He barely knew how to behave, but was smart enough to copy the table manners of the others.

The conversation was rather easy, however, as they asked him about Holland, and very soon he was telling them about the large city of Amsterdam, one of the most important market places in Europe. They asked him how large Holland was and were surprised to hear that France had a much larger area. He also explained that the late King William of Orange had had more power in Holland than in England, although he had only been stadtholder there, a servant of the States General,[40] while he had been king of England. John, encouraged by the easy conversation, asked questions about the mansion. He learned that it was a small property consisting of a few farms and the remains of a small forest. It had a small but beautiful park, which even had a marquee, of which they were very proud. Madame Raboteau explained that the art of landscaping gardens had come from Italy and that an Italian specialist had designed the park. When John expressed his desire to see it, his host was flattered.

"I'm honored that you are interested in our park and would gladly guide you around tomorrow morning. However, I must excuse myself because my duty as governor of Pont-Gibaud makes my presence there necessary. You can still see the park, though. I think that my charming nieces would be better guides than I, anyway. Madame Raboteau will gladly release them from their other duties, I'm sure, in exchange for the privilege of pleasing you."

Thrilled, Madeleine and Jaqueline hastened to express their compliance with their uncle's wish, after Aunt Isabeau had given them permission in a few well chosen words.

The party broke up very soon afterwards, and John was brought to his bedroom after wishing them all a good night's sleep. Uncle Claude and Aunt Isabeau showed their disappointment when the girls left them at the same time. They asked them to stay longer, but the girls declined their invitation, anxious to discuss the possibility of having Mr. Van het Woudt help them out of their predicament, if he was willing. They realized, though, that by talking with him about their plan they were giving themselves away. That could be very dangerous if he was a Romanist. They discussed it without finding a better, less risky approach. At last Jaqueline stated that it was most unlikely they would ever get a better opportunity and must risk it.

"It's an answer to our prayers," she said. Madeleine agreed wholeheartedly but she brought up another difficulty.

---

[40] The Netherlands, the oldest republic in Europe, was ruled by the representatives of its provinces, called the States General.

"How can we talk and explain everything to him, when somebody is following us all the time and will hear every word we say?"

Jaqueline admitted that she didn't know.

"I can't think about it now," she added. "I am too excited to concentrate on it. Anyhow, I get most of my ideas at night, as you know. Let's go to bed. It's quite late, and I'm tired. Everything may look easier tomorrow."

*   *   *

Early the next morning, Jaqueline was the first to wake up. She jumped out of bed and went to the window.

"It's going to be a marvelous day," she muttered, seeing the sun rise in the nearly cloudless sky. "Our walk with Mr. Van het Woudt certainly will be a pleasure, but how can we talk to him secretly?" She remained standing at the window, deep in thought, turning the problem over in her mind. She could think of only one solution: they must find a reason to send the maid back to the mansion. It must be an extremely good reason, she decided, to overrule the strict instructions of her Aunt Isabeau. She considered several possibilities, but not one of them satisfied her completely, until it suddenly dawned on her that the servant would only leave them in an emergency. It took just a few minutes for her to think out a way to create such an emergency.

But it must not occur in the park, she thought. It's too close to the house and doesn't give us enough time to talk to Mr. Van het Woudt. While reconsidering her plan, she made some small changes and finally felt quite confident that it would work.

I've got to do a lot of pretending, though, she considered. For the moment I won't tell Madeleine my plan. If it fails, she can at least truthfully say that she didn't know about it. Happy with her plan to create an emergency and hopeful that it would work, she went over to Madeleine's bed, pulled the cover off and said, "Hurry up, sleepy head. Dress yourself. The early bird catches the worm, and the early girl catches a visitor."

Madeleine stretched herself, yawned, and said, "Good morning, Jaqueline." She added in a whisper, "Did you figure out how to talk with Mr. Van het Woudt?"

"I don't know for sure yet," Jaqueline said softly. "I have a plan, but I must think out the details. Let's wait and see. One never knows, something might come up that'll suit us better. If not, well, then I'll try out one of my wild ideas. We both have to keep our eyes open, though, and take advantage of every opportunity that may occur."

After their morning prayer, which they always did together, the girls dressed, but were interrupted by a knock on the door.

"Who's there?" Madeleine called aloud.

"I'm Marthé, your maid," a voice answered.

"Oh, well, come in," she replied. The door opened and a sturdy girl, much older than the nieces, walked in.

"Madame Raboteau instructed me to wait on both of you this morning. What can I do first?"

"Bring breakfast for us, Marthé, and help us with our hair," Jaqueline commanded promptly. When the girl had left, she commented, "Aunt Isabeau surely picked the best girl for her purpose. It will be hard to get rid of her. I don't even think that our earbobs will tempt her to keep her mouth shut. Well, we can't help it, but you can be sure, Madeleine, that I'll do my utmost to get rid of her."

An hour later the girls were ready. They went down the stairs walking gracefully, as good manners required, followed by Marthé. John, who had been waiting a long time, bowed slightly with his hand on his heart and said, "I'm delighted, *desmoiselles*,[41] that you can find the time to show me around." Both made an elegant curtsey, as they had been taught to do.

"My sister Jaqueline and I love to have this opportunity. I hope you don't mind that we bring our maid, Mr. Van het Woudt?" John, of course, did not have any objections, and soon they

---

[41] Desmoiselles = Young Ladies.

were walking in a dignified manner toward the park. When they were out of sight of the mansion, Jaqueline winked to Madeleine behind John's back, and with a mischievous glint in her eyes addressed John.

"Mr. Van het Woudt, Aunt Isabeau taught us many times that good-mannered ladies always walk slowly with a straight back, and keep up a nice conversation." She began to laugh when she saw John's surprised face, and even more when she saw the puzzled look of Marthé.

"However, Aunt Isabeau has forgotten that it is far more fun to run around than to walk demurely. Please, don't betray us if you think that our behavior is not ladylike. Guess what? I feel like running. Madeleine, you see that fir tree with that broken branch sticking out? Let's see who can get there first. One, two, three . . ." Off the girls went, followed by Marthé.

When John saw the girls running he laughed and also began to sprint toward the fir tree. As soon as they arrived at the tree, Jaqueline began to tease the other two about their performances. Soon all three were laughing and talking together. From that time on, they behaved like good chums, except Marthé, who wasn't sure what she should do.

John, who had been brought up in a large forest, knew a lot about trees. He showed the girls a number of different leaves and told them their names.

Madeleine became quite interested and asked a lot of questions. Jaqueline listened, too, but seemed to like running around better. Often she dashed off ahead of the others, and came back with a leaf, or a bud, and even once with a caterpillar. Marthé, who had indeed been instructed to listen to the girls' conversation, walked a few feet behind Madeleine and John all the time, without hearing anything worthwhile to tell her mistress.

When they arrived in the park, John was disappointed. It was small, slightly more than twenty acres, with young trees, which gave little shadow. The marquee had a nice design, though. The girls explained that it was kept empty and that furniture was only brought to the marquee if a party was given. After strolling through the park a short time, John suggested that they might just as well return to the mansion. Jaqueline disagreed.

"You like old trees, right, Mr. Van het Woudt?" she asked. "The park adjoins the forest on the northern side. I think you may be interested in looking at the trees there." Without waiting for a reply she dashed along the lane toward the forest. They found a small trail twisting its way through the underbrush. At last, Jaqueline felt that they were far enough from the mansion to act out her plan. She rushed ahead of Madeleine and John, and suddenly, with a yell of pain, she stumbled. Madeleine and John saw it happening and ran to help her. When she tried to stand up she fell over again with another cry of pain.

"Ouch, that hurts," she moaned with a painful face while she grabbed her right ankle. "I must have sprained my ankle. I can't stand on it."

"Silly goose, why didn't you watch where to put your feet," scolded Madeleine who had dropped on her knees, and tried to feel if the ankle was swollen.

"Ooow, stop it, I can't stand it. Ow, it hurts," Jaqueline wailed and removed Madeleine's hands from her ankle.

"I'm sorry, darling. Are you sure that it isn't broken?" Madeleine asked.

"I don't think so, but it hurts terribly when I try to move it. As long as I keep it still, I can stand the pain. I can't walk home, though, that is certain!" Jaqueline said contritely.

"Oh, *ma petite*,[42] what can we do?" Madeleine wondered. "How can we get you home?"

At that moment, John who had kept silent in this unusual situation, shrugged his shoulders and said, "It's rather simple. Somebody must go to the mansion and ask for help. They may have a stretcher or can make one and carry her home. I can easily go and be back in an hour." Both girls protested his suggestion. He could not leave them alone, they felt, because nobody knew what could happen in this place.

---

[42] Literally, *My little one* (an affectionate term).

"Yes, I see your point," John agreed. "If I must stay here, Marthé must go, because we need help. What do you think, Marthé, do you know your way back to the mansion?"

Marthé, who had been standing aside, not daring to push herself forward, did not know what to do.

"I know the way back all right, Sir, but I don't know if I'm allowed to go. Madame Raboteau told me to stay with Miss Madeleine and Miss Jaqueline. I will be punished if I leave them alone."

"You won't leave them alone," John said persuasively. "I'll stay with them, and I'll be happy to explain it to your mistress." The girls also urged her to go. At last they convinced her and she reluctantly left.

As soon as Marthé had disappeared, Jaqueline jumped up, and seeing the astonished faces of Madeleine and John, laughed heartily.

"No, no, my ankle isn't hurt at all, but I had to pretend that it was sprained to get rid of Marthé. Madeleine knows why, and we will explain it to you, Mr. Van het Woudt. However, first let us find a more comfortable place to sit. It will take Marthé twenty minutes or so to go home so that we have at least half an hour to explain everything." They went a short distance back, the girls talking and laughing about Jaqueline's idea and found a heavy tree lying on an open, grassy knoll. The girls seated themselves comfortably on the tree and John squatted on the grass, curious to hear the reason for this unexpected development. Jaqueline did not begin directly with their story. First, she wanted to know if she could trust Mr. Van het Woudt.

"Mr. Van het Woudt, do you belong to the Roman Church?" she asked abruptly. Right away, it flashed through John's mind that the girls probably belonged to the Huguenots because he could not imagine a Romanist girl ever asking such a question. Calmly, he told them that he was a Protestant, as were most of the people in Holland, not a Romanist. He added that Jesus was His Savior whom he served.

"Praise the Lord," Madeleine exclaimed. "Didn't we think, Jaqueline, that this could be an answer to our prayers? Oh, Lord, I thank Thee with all my heart!" The joyous expression on Jaqueline's face also clearly showed how excited she was when she directed herself to John again.

"Mr. Van het Woudt, we are two Huguenot girls and in danger of being locked up in a convent. We feel that the Lord purposely brought you here to help us." She began to tell their problem but was interrupted constantly by Madeleine. They explained their plans to run away to England and their problems in finding a skipper. At last they asked John if he would be willing to try to find their old nurse in La Rochelle, and to see if she could hide them until their uncle came from England.

John listened patiently, once in awhile asking a question if something was not clear to him. Like the girls, he felt that the Lord must have sent him to help them. He made up his mind that the search for his father could wait a few days until the girls were safe.

He told the girls that he would help, but that they must hurry and tell him the details of their plan because it would not take long before Marthé would return with some servants. He asked if they could leave the house at night. They replied they couldn't use the main entrance because it was guarded by a footman. However, Madeleine knew the library well and suggested they could climb out of one of its windows without difficulty. After more discussion, it was agreed that John would come back to escort them to safety after he had found a place where the girls could hide, either with their nurse or with someone else. At that moment, Jaqueline suggested that they should go back to the spot where she had supposedly sprained her ankle. But, after they arrived, Jaqueline didn't sit down like the others had expected.

"I've got another problem," she mentioned. "It won't do to have a sprained ankle that looks healthy. It seems to me that it should at least be red and swollen. Let me take care of that while you and Madeleine discuss the rest of our plans."

"What are you going to do?" Madeleine asked.

"I'm going to find a plot of nettles, and then I will rub my ankle thoroughly with them. I don't like it, and am even scared of doing it, but the pain is nothing compared with being discovered." Madeleine and John admired her idea, but felt sorry because of the pain it was sure to cause her.

While she was gone, John and Madeleine discussed how to let them know which night he would be ready to bring them to La Rochelle. After Madeleine admitted that she hadn't the faintest idea how to do it, John smiled and requested one of the ribbons Madeleine had on her bonnet. He promised to attach it to the lowest branch of the tree opposite the main entrance. The following night he would wait for the girls to leave the house. In case something went wrong and the girls could not escape undetected, he would wait a second night.

Since nothing more needed to be discussed, they went in search of Jaqueline. She was just returning with a pained expression on her face and tears in her eyes. Rubbing the nettles on her ankle was far more painful than she had expected. However, it had worked. Madeleine could barely suppress her surprise when she saw the ankle. It was dark red and swollen.

They went back again to the place where Jaqueline had stumbled and sat down. A short time later Marthé arrived with two men, who carried an improvised stretcher.

Without any further adventures, they returned to the mansion where Jaqueline was settled into a chair in her bedroom. A stable boy was waiting with John's horse. After John explained Jaqueline's mishap, he complimented his host on his garden and then left for La Rochelle.

JOHN MEETS THE WASHERWOMAN'S SON

THE first day after his arrival in La Rochelle, John visited the supervisor of the city jail in his office. He was not a gentleman as John had expected, but a heavy set, rough-looking man without manners and with little education. The supervisor's attitude became rather cool when he heard that John was Dutch because it was well known in La Rochelle that the Dutch were the arch enemies of the Sun King. When John, however, purposely mentioned that he had spoken with Chevalier de Langeron, the captain of La Palme, and that he was on a special assignment for the French government in Paris, the supervisor was clearly impressed and became quite friendly.

During the exchange of polite pleasantries that followed John's introduction, he learned that the prison was relatively empty, since a large group of convicts had been transferred to Lyon, just three days earlier. John, surprised that they were transported away from the sea to an inland city, asked impulsively why these convicts, who were trained to row on war galleys, were sent to Lyon, where they couldn't be used efficiently. The supervisor, enjoying his talk with the Dutch foreigner, explained that their final destination was Marseille, the harbor in southern France. The large detour was needed to pick up more convicts. They would collect them from each city prison they passed, so that a large group would finally arrive in Marseille, where they were badly needed on a newly built galley. With a cruel smile on his face, he added that these criminals would be footsore after having walked for three or four weeks. It didn't matter, though, because they would be sitting on the rowers' bench for the rest of their miserable lives. John had a hard time remaining unemotional when he heard these heartless words, but he managed a thin smile. With a feigned nonchalance, he remarked casually that Chevalier de Langeron probably would be interested to know if all the convicts he had left behind, including the cursed Huguenots, belonged to that group.

"Oh, yes," the supervisor assured him, "Not only they, but I also send along every convict who serves a life term. It saves the city a lot of money when we don't have to feed them anymore."

After a few more polite sentences, John bid him goodbye, and left the supervisor's office, who wondered for the rest of the day why that foreign gentleman had taken the trouble to visit him.

John reflected, while he walked to the inn where he was staying, that his father most likely belonged to that group of convicts being sent to Marseille. He had just missed him. It would be best to follow the convict transport directly. He couldn't do that, though, because the Raboteau girls had to be helped first. He comforted himself with the thought that a week's delay did not matter. It would be easy to get ahead of the convicts. They were walking slowly over a large detour whereas he was on horseback and could go via a shorter route.

After eating lunch, he called for the innkeeper and asked him if there was a woman who could wash his linen. He added that he had heard of a Mrs. Duval, who was supposed to be one of the best washerwomen in La Rochelle. The face of the innkeeper showed his surprise that her name was known by a foreign traveler.

"We have several excellent washerwomen in La Rochelle, Sir," he answered politely. "I don't know exactly where Mrs. Duval is living, but if you would like to use her service, I can easily find out and send one of my girls with your linen to her."

"You don't know the Dutch very well, I think," John said smiling. "Were you never told that the Dutch are very particular as far as clean linen is concerned? I certainly want to know what kind of soap she'll be using before I trust her with my linen. By all means, send your servant to tell her to pick up my linen herself. Please, hurry. I don't want to wait for her all day. She can find me in your garden."

A huge oak tree shaded most of the garden. In its shadow stood a rough hewn table and a few chairs. He had not been in the garden before, but had assumed that it was the best place for his meeting. He was pleased to see that he had been right. Anyone trying to overhear them would be visible. Relaxed, he sat down on one of the benches and put his feet on the table.

He soon fell asleep, but was suddenly wakened by a woman's soft voice.

"Excuse me, Sir. Are you the gentleman who wants his linen cleaned?"

He turned around and saw a small woman with a friendly face standing close behind him.

"Are you Mrs. Duval, the washerwoman?"

"Yes, I am," the woman replied.

"Listen carefully," John said in a subdued tone. "Do you know the Raboteau girls? They are in danger and need help."

The woman clasped her hands together in sudden fear and replied with a happy, but scared voice, "Wouldn't I know Jacqueline and Madeleine, my girls? Nobody knows them better than I, who was their nurse for nearly ten years. Oh, Sir, what is wrong with the darlings? They're with their aunt and uncle, aren't they?"

"Mrs. Duval, I want to talk with you about it as soon as possible, but not here. It's too dangerous. The girls told me that you are a Huguenot. Is that true, or have you also become a New Convert? May I come to your house tonight, and is your husband to be trusted?"

The woman made a gesture of fright and glanced furtively over her shoulder, but when she saw that nobody could have overheard the foreigner, she became calm again.

"The girls were right. I am still a Huguenot. My husband went to be with the Lord three years ago, and I live in a small house alone where you cannot meet me without drawing the attention of the whole neighborhood." She thought a few moments, and then told John, "Meet me at my son Matthieu's place. He is a grape grower and his house will be easy to find. It's the fifth house on the right side of the road going outside the eastern city gate."

John, pleased that the woman had reacted so sensibly, told her that he would be at her son's house late in the afternoon.

"Excuse me, Sir. I cannot be there in time to tell him you are coming. Tomorrow is Sunday and I will visit him as usual. You may then come any time of the day, but the road is nearly deserted early in the morning and that may be the safest time for you," Mrs. Duval said. She nodded resolutely, and John, aware that he had forgotten the Lord's day, blushed. He hastened to tell that he would be there the next morning. Knowing that a long talk would seem suspicious to the innkeeper, he broke off the conversation abruptly. He held his small parcel of dirty linen out to Mrs. Duval who took it, bowed slightly, turned and left the garden.

*   *   *

Matthieu's house was easy to find. It was a dilapidated, old shack, which in former times probably had served as a barn. A few scrawny chickens were scratching in the soil of the overgrown yard in an effort to find some food. The shanty stood on the edge of a large vineyard, which, unlike the house, was well kept. In front of the house next to the open door sat a young man, poorly dressed, leaning with his back against the wooden wall. When he saw John turning in toward the house, he stood up, took off his cap, and waited humbly for John to address him.

"Are you Matthieu, Mrs. Duval's son?" John asked.

"Yes, I am," the young man responded. "My mother told me that you were coming. She is inside waiting for you. Please, let me tie up your horse behind the house. It is better if he can't be seen easily from the road."

John dismounted and gave the rein to Matthieu, who looked him full in his face and said slowly, "I want to know more about you before you can enter the house. My mother expects you to be a Huguenot because you are willing to help the Raboteau girls. Is that true? Are you one of our brothers in Christ? How can I be certain that you aren't lying?"

"Yes, I belong to Christ. I am a Huguenot who fled to Holland and have returned for a short time. I cannot prove it. I can only give my word that I am not lying," John replied earnestly. Matthieu looked a few moments in his face and then began to smile.

"I believe you," he said simply. "You may go into the house. My mother is there and some of my friends, brothers in Christ. We have waited with our Sunday morning worship service for you."

The door opened into a large room with several men and women. Even a few teenage boys and girls were sitting on benches along the walls. An older man with gray hair stood up and came to John.

"Our sister Duval told us that you are one of our brothers in Christ from Holland. Be welcome in the name of the Lord. As you know, it is dangerous to come together for this worship service, but we trust that you won't tell anyone. We'll begin as soon as brother Matthieu comes in. Please, seat yourself." John thanked him politely, excused himself and turned, smiling, to Mrs. Duval who was sitting on the other side of the room.

"I'm happy to meet you here, Mrs. Duval, even more so because I now have the opportunity to meet the other brothers and sisters." He looked around and became aware that all of them were listening, so he added, "As you all know I am now living in Holland, and can assure you that the Dutch know about the suffering of the church in France. They are helping as much as they can. As a matter of fact, I expect to return there shortly and am willing to take any verbal messages with me, if needed." Mrs. Duval replied, smiling, "I'm happy I wasn't mistaken. I don't think that you have to take any messages for we correspond with the Scottish church on a regular basis. However, we can talk more about it after the service."

At this moment, Matthieu returned and remained standing in the middle of the room. The old man who had waited patiently while John was talking with Mrs. Duval now brought him to a bench where he seated John next to himself.

The small congregation, not having a minister, was led by Matthieu and the worship service showed that he was well suited for it. His simple words were a comfort to all of them who belonged to the "church in the desert."[43] John felt especially encouraged because Matthieu talked about the words of the apostle Paul who said that absolutely nothing can separate us from the love of God which is in Christ Jesus, our Lord.[44] He perceived that Matthieu knew about the transportation of the galley slaves to Lyon, for he prayed fervently for these brothers who were suffering for Christ's sake.

All of them stayed after the service, talking with each other and John. Obviously, they were anxious to know about the Huguenots in Holland, and John wanted to know about La Rochelle.

"Are there other Huguenots in La Rochelle?" he asked during their conversation, because he knew that it had been a stronghold of the Huguenots in the past.

"Yes. A few more are living in other parts of the city, but we can't come together in larger groups anymore for fear of being discovered and punished," Matthieu explained. However, they agreed that these "inconveniences," as they called them, were nothing compared with the suffering of their brothers on the galleys, and the Church in the south of France. Many of them had been murdered, they said.

Gradually, all of them left except Mrs. Duval, Matthieu, and the old man, who appeared to be respected as an elder. During and after their simple noon meal John told them how he had come in contact with Madeleine and Jaqueline Raboteau. He mentioned that he intended to help them and urged the others to do the same. Matthieu confirmed that the girls' uncle,

---

[43] The Huguenots called their church "The church in the wilderness" (desert) based on Revelation 12, persecuted by the dragon, but preserved by the Lord.

[44] Romans 8:38, 39.

Jean Charles, a Huguenot, had fled to Scotland, but regularly came to La Rochelle. He loaded his boat with either grapes or apples, depending on the season, which he resold in England. By doing this, he was able to be the contact man between the Huguenots in La Rochelle, and the Protestants in Scotland.

In fact, Matthieu knew him well because he always delivered most of his grapes to him. They expected him to be in the harbor of La Rochelle within a week to pick up the first load of apples for that year. Mrs. Duval and Matthieu were convinced that he would do his utmost to help his nieces to get to England. After some more talk, Matthieu and the old man both felt that they could borrow two horses for a few days for the girls to use.

"Don't expect riding horses," Matthieu warned, "These are farm horses used for plowing and drawing farm carts. Saddles won't fit their broad backs, but that is not too bad because their backs are comfortable to sit on, especially for two girls riding on the same horse."

"Why do we need the other horse then?" John asked. "I've got my own horse, and one for the girls would be enough."

"Well, I'm going with you and I need a horse too, don't you think? It would be foolish for you to go alone. How do you expect to find your way in the dark? I'm a pretty good guide. I know all the small lanes and trails in the country like the back of my own hand. Besides, two men are always better than one if things don't work out," Matthieu replied quietly.

After more discussion, John and Matthieu agreed to go together to help the girls escape the mansion. Their plan was simple. Leaving Monday afternoon, they would most likely return on Thursday. Matthieu would bring the girls to his mother, who would hide them until they could board the ship. He would also contact Mr. Jean Charles Raboteau, the skipper, as soon as he arrived. The rest would be child's play, they thought.

12

ESCAPE FROM THE MANSION

JOHN and Matthieu left for the mansion just after sundown. Matthieu, sitting bareback on a large farm horse, rode in front leading another horse for the girls. John followed on his own horse. It was difficult riding in the dark night with only the light of the stars. The tiniest sliver of moon showed for a short time, but it was not enough to make the trip easier. It was so dark that John couldn't see Matthieu and could only follow the same path by relying on his ears. His horse did not need any guidance, though. He simply let the reins hang loosely and the animal followed close behind the others.

Matthieu knew the country thoroughly. All night long he guided John along country lanes and bypaths until they arrived at the mansion just before sunrise. Matthieu rode to the beginning of a small trail that led to the front stairs, as he told John in whispers. While he held the horses, John followed the trail on foot, stepping carefully so that he made no unnecessary noise. Matthieu was right. The trail ended close to the tree in front of the house. His arrival there could not have been better timed. The first rays of the sun were just coming above the horizon, giving enough light to find the lowest branch, to which he attached the ribbon as he had agreed upon with the girls. After his return to Matthieu, he found him ready to take off again. With a low voice, John mentioned that the ribbon was in place and without saying more, he followed Matthieu away from the mansion.

Matthieu brought him to an empty barn in a field, far enough from the mansion to feel safe. All day long they rested, slept, and talked, mainly about the suffering of the Church of Christ in France. Matthieu explained that few ministers were left. Many had been killed or condemned to serve a life term rowing on the galleys. Some had escaped to England or Holland. He mentioned also that the king had sent a new governor, Lamoignon de Bâville, with a large detachment of troops to the southern part of France. He and his soldiers were hunting down the followers of Christ as if they were vermin. Men, women, and children were killed everywhere.

During their talk, John began to understand that Matthieu could have left France several times, but had refused to consider these opportunities. He was convinced that he was needed for the few Christians who were in the worship service. Hearing this, John began more and more to trust and respect him. During that day, he confided to Matthieu under the seal of secrecy who he was and why he had returned to France. He even told him his real name. Matthieu listened quietly, and remarked that when he heard that John was a Huguenot, he had already guessed that he had come with a special mission. When John mentioned his plan to go to the south in search of his father, Matthieu cautioned him. The situation there was far more dangerous than in any other part of France, he explained.

That night they returned to the mansion. John waited patiently under the tree for the girls while Matthieu held the horses ready at the beginning of the trail.

Again, it was pitch dark and John couldn't see a thing, but he didn't mind, though. It was a quiet night. The wind barely moved the leaves of the trees and the few night animals could hardly be heard. Therefore, he expected to hear the girls when they came down the stairs.

For a long time nothing happened. Then, all at once he heard somewhere to the left of the front stairs the sound of a door or window being opened, followed by the plop of somebody falling. He quietly moved in the direction of the sound, but before he had found the place where it had occurred, he heard an exited whispering followed by the sound of another plop. John moved as fast as he could in the dark, with his arms in front of his face to protect himself against the branches. Apparently, he miscalculated the distance he needed to go, for he collided with somebody. He heard a subdued cry of pain and recognized Madeleine's voice.

"It's I, Mr. Van het Woudt. Is that you, Miss Madeleine?" he whispered.

"Yes, and Jaqueline is here also," she replied. He told Madeleine to hold his hand and to give her hand to Jaqueline. In this way, it was easy to guide them to Matthieu and the horses.

After Matthieu was introduced to the girls, he showed them the horse they had to ride together and apologized that it was a farm horse without a saddle. They laughed and said that it didn't matter. When they tried to mount the horse, they discovered, however, that the horse was too tall for them to mount alone. John, feeling their embarrassment more than seeing it, offered to help them. He folded his hands, and let the girls use it as a step. It worked, but the girls had a hard time keeping their balance on the horse's slippery back. When they said so, Matthieu promised to go as slowly as possible.

They continued riding all night long and arrived without accident at daybreak at Matthieu's cottage. The girls were brought inside and stayed there while John had a serious talk with Matthieu who promised to bring the girls to his mother that same day. When John objected that it would be too dangerous in daytime, Matthieu explained that it must be done. His mother's house was in La Rochelle and the gates would be closed at night.

"Don't worry, John," he said while he grinned mischievously, "I didn't borrow just two horses, but a cart as well. It would be foolish not to use this opportunity to bring some supplies to my mother. She needs some flour, butter, and eggs, and I will also give her a barrel of wine, which is quite common because I am well known as a grape grower. One of the girls will be hidden between the supplies, and the other one, dressed as a peasant girl, can walk next to the cart, or even sit on it without drawing any attention."

"Well, it sounds safer than I thought and I see no other possibility," John agreed. "Be careful, though, for it would be disastrous for the girls to be caught now. You told me that a few years ago a new law was made so that women and girls can be punished like men. I am worried, Matthieu. These lovely girls will be whipped cruelly if they are caught.

"That brings up another matter I'd like to talk about. The most dangerous time for the girls is when they are on board ship before leaving the harbor. I intend to be there to help if something unforeseen would happen. Matthieu, I'd like you to help also. We agreed that you will explain the situation to skipper John Charles. The day after his arrival, I'll go to the harbor, find him and ask for passage to England. If he is willing to take the girls as you expect, he must take me also! He'll know the best time for me to go aboard, most likely before the girls arrive.

"In the morning of that day you must come to the inn where I'm staying and ask for my horse. I want to make the impression that the horse is sold and that I will not return to France. In reality, you must agree with the skipper to put me secretly ashore at night some distance south of La Rochelle where you must be waiting with my horse so that I can continue my journey. Don't you think that's the right thing to do, Matthieu?"

"Yes, I think so," Matthieu agreed with a serious expression. "For the moment the girls are safe, but I'm sure that a thorough search will be made when it is discovered that they have gone. Obviously, all ships leaving the harbor will be searched. Your presence may help, provided that you aren't under suspicion yourself. I can't judge that, but I'm willing to do my part. Your plan sounds good to me." They understood each other well. Both were willing to risk their life and they didn't want to elaborate further. After an affectionate handshake, John took his horse and returned to the city, glad that the first part of their plan was completed.

*   *   *

John had to wait two days for a ship to arrive from England. He had already told the innkeeper of his plan to cross over to England provided he could find a good ship. It was an excellent excuse for spending most of his time at the waterfront looking at the few ships and asking questions about their destinations. The second day he saw a ship entering the harbor that proudly flew the English flag. Rigged with only a few sails, it glided slowly toward the quay, where it dropped its anchor.

John realized that if the skipper was Jean Charles, he should not draw attention before Matthieu had talked with him. On the other hand, it was important to know as soon as possible if this ship was the one they were looking for. He decided there was nothing wrong with asking, as long as he did it casually and not as if he was really interested.

Up ahead he saw two older men sitting on a pile of wood. They looked like old sailors and he assumed that they could tell him more about this newly arrived ship. He casually strolled toward them with his hands folded behind his back, stopped a moment and remarked, without addressing anyone in particular, "Nice ship, that new one. I wonder where it comes from?" The old men looked at him curiously but did not say anything. Somewhat disappointed about their lack of response, he addressed them directly.

"Isn't that a ship from England? That doesn't happen very often here, does it?"

"No, Sir, it doesn't. It is the *Hope and Glory* from Dublin, a large fishing boat used for trading." John smiled contemptuously and remarked that he didn't see what goods an Englishman could find for trading, France being as poor as it was. The other man agreed with him, but said that the skipper of this ship was French himself and had a special license for trading. He came frequently to purchase grapes, wine, or apples which he sold in England.

"Well, the skipper must be a smart fellow making lots of money by selling the excellent French wine to the English," he remarked offhand and turned to go to the inn again.

"He is certainly a smart one, young Raboteau. He was born and bred here and we know his whole family. All of them are bright," John heard the sailor say. He didn't stop but waved an amiable goodbye, grinning because now he knew all he wanted to know.

∗   ∗   ∗

"Yes, Sir, I can give you passage to London, if that's convenient for you," said skipper Jean Charles Raboteau, a sturdy young man with an open face. His voice was loud and his eyes kept watch over the few men bringing large, heavy barrels aboard.

"You may use my cabin while we are at sea. We'll leave the day after tomorrow and you'll have to pay me ten francs[45] before we set sail. You have to bring your own provisions for I don't provide any meals. I suggest that you come aboard early tonight. That will save you the cost of sleeping at an inn. Hold on," he suddenly yelled, running forward, just in time to put his back against a barrel the men nearly let slip through their hands.

"Careful now, boys," he said encouragingly while they slowly let the barrel slide into the hold after which he came back to John, wiping the perspiration from his forehead.

"I'm sorry, Sir, but I've no time to discuss it any longer. Are you coming or not?" John said that he accepted his offer, but the skipper barely listened, giving the loading all of his attention.

That afternoon, when John was sitting at ease in the garden of the inn enjoying the nice weather, the innkeeper appeared with his cap in his hand.

"Sir, a man has come to take your horse away. You want me to give him the horse or do you want to see him first?"

"I'd like to have a word with him," John replied. "Please, bring him here."

A few moments later the innkeeper returned with a man who held his cap politely in his hand. John recognized him as one of the brothers whom he had seen in the worship service, and realized that Matthieu felt it safer not to come himself, but had sent him to act as a servant.

---

[45] Ten francs was slightly less than one week's wages for a skilled laborer.

"Tell your master that the innkeeper is willing to vouch that the horse is in excellent condition, right?" John said, waiting for the innkeeper to answer, who willingly confirmed it.

"Please also give this man the saddle and all the gear that belongs to the horse," John told the innkeeper. Next, he turned to the servant.

"Give my regards to your master and make sure that the groom takes good care of the horse. Here is some money to quench your thirst on the road." John took three sous[46] out of his pocket and gave them to the man. The servant thanked him humbly and went to the stables with the innkeeper.

---

[46] One sou corresponds to approximately two U.S. dollars in modern times.

13

THE HARBOR MASTER

THE skipper and his men were still busy stowing away the cargo when John boarded the ship late in the afternoon. Jean Charles hurriedly showed him his cabin and told him to make himself at home. Before leaving John alone he whispered that they would talk more that night.

The cabin wasn't very big. It contained a small table attached to the floor, a chair, a bench attached to one of the walls and a narrow cot attached to another wall. John put his valise under the cot and went to the deck to look at all the commotion.

When, a few hours later, it became too dark to work Jean Charles sent the men to a sailors inn. He told them that he had paid for a meal and didn't need them until the next morning. They all took off like happy children who are promised free candy, while Jean Charles and John retreated to the cabin. The skipper lit a candle, and with a gesture of his hand invited John to sit on the bench.

"At last we have time to get better acquainted," he said. "I talked with Matthieu last night and he told me to expect you this morning. As you see, I've sent my people away, mainly because my nieces may arrive any time now." While he was talking they heard some noise outside. The cabin door opened and two figures draped in black walked in, followed by Matthieu.

"Well, girls, it's safe to take off your cloaks now," Matthieu said cheerfully. "Let me introduce you to your uncle Jean Charles." The girls were wrapped in long black cloaks and wore hoods fashioned from large, black scarfs, which they held tightly over their heads. They threw their disguises off and turned to Jean Charles in happy relief.

"We are so pleased to meet you, Uncle Jean Charles," Madeleine said. Looking to the others, she continued, "We don't know how to thank you all for the risks you are willing to take for our sake. We thank the Lord continuously for helping us so well." Spontaneously she embraced her uncle and Jaqueline followed her example. Upon hearing Matthieu tell John that he had to leave she turned to Matthieu and hugged him too.

"Matthieu, I don't know how to show you our gratitude. May the Lord bless you. I hope that some day we'll meet again in England. *Adieu*."[47] Madeleine also hugged him, expressing her gratitude in no uncertain terms.

Matthieu, taken aback, muttered something like, "I couldn't have done less," and then regained his composure.

"I've got to go now, girls," he said somewhat louder. "I'm happy that I was allowed to help a little. May the Lord give you the freedom you desire so much. Jean Charles, please, take good care of them. John, I'll see you a few nights hence. Goodbye, all of you," and he stumbled through the door and disappeared in the darkness.

"Let's sit down," Jean Charles said after the cabin door had been closed. "We don't have too much time because my men will return soon. Girls, you can sit on the cot, John on the bench, and I'll take the chair. Well, well, girls, you've changed a lot since I last saw you four years ago. You've surely grown up and are a credit to the Church of Christ, making the proper choice under these circumstances. We'll do our utmost to get you safely to England. What has happened with my brother Claude? I can't understand why he has changed so much." During the next five minutes the girls began to talk about the different events, but very soon Jean Charles interrupted them.

"The rest of your stories will have to wait, girls. We don't have time anymore. We've got to make plans on how to keep you safe tomorrow because it will probably be the most dangerous day of your life. We can't sail unless we get the permission of

---

[47] *Adieu* = goodbye (literally: to God).

the harbor master. He'll give a permit only after he has searched the ship to make sure that we aren't smuggling Huguenots to England. We'll have to hide you, girls, so that he won't find you. The problem is that this ship is fairly small, without good hiding places. I was unable to figure out where to put you until I took one of my men, the ship's carpenter, a staunch Presbyterian, into my confidence. He came up with an excellent idea. We are loaded with apples. Some of them are loose, but most are packed in barrels. He suggested hiding you both in two barrels, which he changed for this purpose. Come, John, help me carry one of them into the cabin so we can have a look at it."

They left and returned a few minutes later with an empty barrel. The girls saw that the round bottom end was missing and that the top had been moved inside the barrel so that the ends of the bulging side planks and the round top made a kind of open container. "It is obviously too cumbersome to put the girls into a barrel and nail the top and bottom shut. After all, they must be able to get out in an emergency. This barrel is better suited to our purpose. If one of the girls sits on the floor, we can place the barrel over her, and fill the top with apples. It will be a perfect hiding place. What do you think, John?"

"I agree, provided some holes are drilled in the top to get enough air for breathing. Besides, the barrels must be tied up so that they cannot topple over," John said, after considering the barrel.

"The carpenter can drill the holes as soon as he comes back. I would suggest that one barrel will be tied up in the corner of this cabin, and the other one to the mast. We can say that the apples are for you, John, and for the sailors during the crossing over to England. I'll forbid my people, of course, to take food or apples before we have cast off for England. Well, girls, who will be sitting at the mast and who will stay in the cabin?"

"It doesn't make that much difference to me," Jaqueline said. "You prefer the cabin, don't you, Madeleine?" After Madeleine nodded her agreement, Jean Charles ended the conversation quickly.

"You girls don't have to hide now. Both of you can sleep on the cot. John and I will sleep outside and discuss our plans for tomorrow. As soon as the carpenter comes, I'll put him to work. Tomorrow morning, just before sunrise, we'll put you both into the barrels and you must stay there until either John or I tell you to come out. Good night, girls. We will certainly pray for your well-being tomorrow. John, please help me put the barrel into the corner."

After moving the barrel, they went to the deck, leaving the girls alone to get some sleep.

*   *   *

It was still dark the next morning, when John, accompanied by a short, stocky man, knocked on the cabin door. Having waited for some time without any response, he assumed that the girls were afraid to answer, and opened the door. It was true, as Jaqueline admitted readily, they had not known who it was and were scared that it could be a stranger. John introduced his partner as Duncan, the carpenter, who muttered something the girls didn't understand. He went to the barrel and began to drill holes into the upper lid. When he was ready, he told John in a mixture of Scottish, English, and French that he was going to do the same to the other barrel and left the cabin.

John told the girls that he wanted to find out if the sailors were still asleep, and left too. Very soon he returned with Duncan and the skipper. Jean Charles said cheerfully, "Now, Madeleine, if you sit down in this corner we'll place the barrel over you. Don't be frightened when you hear Duncan hammering away. He must put a few nails into the wall of the cabin so that we can tie the barrel to the wall." Madeleine came forward, but John stopped her.

"You shouldn't sit down on the floor. Take this pillow from the cot, so you'll be more comfortable." Madeleine thanked him, sat down on the pillow with her knees pulled up, and the men placed the barrel over her, tying it down with a rope to

. . . the men placed the barrel over her, tying it down . . .

the nails in the wall. Jean Charles and Duncan went out and came back with a basket of apples, which they emptied into the top container of the barrel.

"Duncan, your idea is excellent. Nobody would expect a girl to be in this barrel," John complimented Duncan, who thanked him with a smile. Next, the men disappeared with Jaqueline to place her in the barrel, tied to the mast. After that was done, all was ready for the ship's inspection by the harbor master and his men.

John went back to the cabin. After telling Madeleine that he was going to sit outside the cabin waiting for the inspectors, he picked up his chair and placed it next to the door opening. He sat down and leaned leisurely against the cabin wall, whistling a tune between his teeth. He made a perfect picture of a rich young man without a care in the world. The first few hours, nothing happened. The men, supervised by the skipper, were making everything ready for sailing. Then, all at once, the skipper was called away, and a few moments later he came to John with three men. Two of them stayed in the background but the third one, an uniformed man with a commanding air, walked next to the skipper.

"Mr. Van het Woudt forgive me for intruding on your time. I would like to introduce the harbor master, Mr. Benoit," Jean Charles said politely.

"Mr. Benoit, this is Mr. Van het Woudt, a passenger who rented my cabin for this trip to England. He is representing the Dutch government, with a special recommendation of one of the ministers of His Majesty, our King." Without changing his carefree, indifferent attitude, John said haughtily to the harbor master, "It is a pleasure to meet you, Sir; what can I do for you?" The harbor master turned to his men and ordered them to start searching the ship and to report to him when they were done. After they were gone, he turned to John, whom he had scrutinized during the introduction of the skipper.

"I'd like to see your credentials, Sir," he requested politely but coolly.

"What a nuisance," John said contemptuously, but he took out of his breast pocket his letter of recommendation and handed it to the harbor master. The officer read it carefully, handed it back to John and bowed slightly.

"Sir, it is my duty to search the skipper's cabin and to read essential data from the logbook. I request your permission to do my duty." John nodded his permission and waited when the harbor master looked around and took the logbook from the table drawer. Next, he thanked John in official terms for having given his permission and left. After he was gone, John removed his shoes and lay down on the cot for a rest. He heard the usual noise of sailors moving around the cargo until, after a few hours, the noise became far less. A short time later he heard one of the harbor master's men going around yelling, "All hands must leave ship. All hands must leave ship."

This was the preparation for the fumigation of the ship,[48] a process Jean Charles and John feared most because both girls would be poisoned if they could not prevent it. They had spent considerable time working out a plan in which John had to play the main role. He turned on his side with his face toward the cabin and pretended to sleep.

Some men going toward the hatch that led to the cargo underneath the deck, were suddenly interrupted by the loud voice of the skipper.

"Stop it, men! You can't burn the gas while Mr. Van het Woudt is in his cabin. Don't you have any common sense?" After some murmuring, which John could not understand, the voice of the skipper thundered, "Stand still, I tell you for the last time. One more step and I'll kick you overboard." The next words sounded as if he had turned his head toward the wall.

---

[48] When the government of King Louis XIV discovered that many Huguenots escaped across the sea to England and Holland they established during the latter part of the seventeenth century the rule that all ships leaving the harbor had to be fumigated with poison gas.

"Duncan, Come here! Hurry up, please! Come aboard!" After a few heavy, fast footsteps, the skipper was heard again.

"One of you go to the harbor master and tell him that I refuse to have the ship fumigated as long as Mr. Van het Woudt is in his cabin. I don't have the authority to order him ashore. Mr. Benoit must come himself to force him off the ship. Duncan, you keep an eye on that guy. If he makes any undesired movement, just push him into the harbor!"

"Aye, aye, Sir," he heard Duncan reply phlegmatically.

It was quiet for a long time. At last John heard several footsteps coming toward the cabin. He kept his eyes closed and made the impression of being completely relaxed, although he felt so nervous that he barely could keep his hands still. The cabin door opened, John looked up, yawned and slowly took a seating position as if he had just woken up. He rubbed his eyes and frowned when he saw the skipper and the harbor master both standing at the door of the cabin.

"Mr. Raboteau, I paid an exorbitant price for this cabin and demand to be left alone. I was disturbed a few hours ago, and that was not what I paid for. I want you and the harbor master to get out and not disturb me again."

"Mr. Van het Woudt," the harbor master cut in, "We both serve our gracious king and we both have our instructions. My instruction is not to give permission to any ship to leave the harbor until poison gas has been put in its hold and cabins. I gave orders that every one must leave the ship before this is done. Why don't you obey the instructions of our gracious king?"

John slowly put his legs outside the cot and eased himself into a comfortable position.

"Mr. Raboteau," he said haughtily," I don't need you anymore. This intrusion on my time wasn't your fault. Mr. Benoit, please, sit down and let's discuss the problem." The skipper disappeared and the harbor master came forward a few steps into the room but did not sit down.

"Well, Mr. Benoit, how long does this poisoning procedure last? Forgive me for not knowing about such simple things but I was never exposed to such ridiculous measures."

"Releasing the gas takes about half an hour, but it is better to stay out of the ship for at least six hours because it may take that long before all the air pockets have fresh air again," Mr. Benoit replied reluctantly. He suspected the conversation was not going in the proper direction.

"You want me to leave this ship for more than six hours?" John asked, astonished. "What's the matter with your people? They searched the whole ship! Aren't they smart enough to discover any possible hiding place? Phooey, I would train my men better!"

"My men did a good job," Mr. Benoit said, defending his men, "but it's the law, the command of the king. My instructions are clear. I have to fumigate the ship. You must clear the cabin but I can easily get a room for you in an inn during the poisoning process."

"Well, I don't intend to leave this ship and go to an inn. It isn't convenient," John said shortly. "You aren't aware, Mr. Benoit, that insulting the Dutch government by commanding me to leave ship, isn't in your best interest. This is especially true now when the relationship between my government and his majesty, the king, is strained."

"I can't do anything else than follow my instructions, even if you run a large risk by not leaving the ship. The skipper can testify that I gave you ample warning," Mr. Benoit replied stubbornly.

"Oh, you are mistaken," John said in a conciliatory tone. "Of course I would rather go to an inn than be fumigated, but you've got to take the consequences. I will certainly report to Seigneur de Pontchartrain in Paris how you interpret his instructions to give me any help possible. Wake up, Mr. Benoit. Your instructions weren't given for me. This ship is an exception in your general instructions. I understand it's hard for you to make a decision. After all, you have engaged your people and must pay them for their time even if they don't work. Well, I'm willing to pay a small sum to solve your problem and be left alone."

John grabbed into his pocket, and took out five Louis d'Ors.[49] "This will help you pay your men and buy them an extra drink."

John, pretending to be bored, waited anxiously for Mr. Benoit's reply. If he didn't take the bribe, he knew that everything would be lost.

Mr. Benoit's face had changed drastically. First, he looked distressed that he was placed in such a dilemma. When John mentioned money, his face brightened at the thought of making money without any risk because he knew that John's letter of recommendation would let him off scot-free.

"I'll withdraw my men, Sir. Mr. Raboteau can get his permit at my office. I wish you a safe crossover, Sir," Mr. Benoit said, leaving the cabin.

A few minutes later, John heard the harbor master's men leave and the sailors return aboard. He forced himself to stay in the cabin until he heard the anchor being lifted and felt the ship beginning to move.

When he came on deck, the wind was filling the sails and the skipper, standing at the steering wheel, welcomed him with a broad smile. They agreed it was best to let the girls stay in the barrels until the harbor was out of sight, which did not take long.

First, they released Jaqueline who told them that it had been boring, sitting in a cramped position without hearing anything. Madeleine had a different opinion. She had heard the whole conversation and did not hide her admiration for John, who had played his role so convincingly. Excitedly, she told her sister what had happened and both were thrilled, knowing full well that John had risked his life to gain their freedom.

*   *   *

---

[49] Five Louis d'Ors represented approximately two month wages for a skilled laborer.

It was close to midnight when John and the skipper had their last meeting. After leaving the harbor, Jean Charles had turned the ship to the south to bring John to the place where Matthieu would be waiting with his horse. The Raboteau sisters were sleeping quietly on the cot in the cabin, unaware that John was leaving. He didn't want to say goodbye to them, realizing how difficult this would be after everything they had done together. In his last talk, he entrusted Jean Charles with his address in Holland and urged him to write and tell him how the girls made out and where they were staying.[50]

When the ship arrived at the place where Matthieu was waiting, Duncan and another sailor hauled the rowboat close enough to the ship so that John and the skipper could easily get aboard. Two of the sailors rowed them silently to the beach. A short distance from the dry sand, the boat ran aground, as could be expected. At the command of the skipper, one of the sailors stepped in the water, and told John to climb on his back so that he could get ashore dry footed. Matthieu wasn't there, but the skipper assured John that they were at the right place and that Matthieu would turn up as if nothing had happened. He gave John his valise, and, after an affectionate goodbye to John, returned to the boat. The rowboat disappeared in the darkness. First, John heard the noise of the oars, then the boarding of the ship and a few moments later everything was quiet again.

---

[50] The Raboteau girls did well in their newly adopted country. One of them married Alderman Peter Barre, whose son was the famous Isaac Barre, Member of Parliament and Privy Councillor. The other married Mr. Stephen Chaigneau. Several of their descendants have filled important offices in the state, army, and the Church of England and Ireland.

14
CAPTURED!

SLOWLY the horse walked along the road, visibly tired after a long day. John patted him encouragingly on his shoulder while looking around for a good resting place. Slightly ahead where the road turned more closely to the river, a beautiful, majestic oak tree stood in a large meadow. He steered the horse to it and dismounted. The grass was thick and green and would make a comfortable sleeping place.

Without hurrying he took the saddle from the horse and led him to the water for a good drink. Next, he exchanged the bridle for a halter with a long rope and tied the horse to the tree.

"No bran for you today, Prince," he said, affectionately. "Grass is good enough for you. Be happy: the end of our journey is coming. One or two more days, and we may soon meet Dad."

He felt tired and stiff from the long days of traveling, so he stretched his legs by walking around a short time. Then he went to the river for a drink, and finished off by eating a piece of bread and a few apples from the food stored in his saddlebag. For two weeks he had forced himself to travel ten hours daily toward Marseille. Twice during the trip, his horse had become so exhausted that it had been necessary to trade him in for another one at a post house. Both times he had demanded and gotten the best horse of the stable, thanks to the recommendation of the Minister of Finance. Some nights, including last night, he had stayed in an inn, more for his horse's benefit than for himself. During the rest of his journey he had slept in the open, wrapped in his saddle blanket. The weather had been warm, without rain, and it was safer this way. It was also cheaper.

Yes, he decided, after thinking it over, he had done well, better than he had initially expected.

He went to sleep just before sunset, after making sure that the horse could not pull itself loose.

He did not know how long he had slept, but suddenly he woke up, frightened. Several hands were grabbing him and trying to turn him over, pulling his hands behind his back. Some were also holding his legs, tying them with a rope. He was not sure what was happening, but in a wild rage he fought back, kicking and hitting, twisting and wriggling like a snake. It did not help much. Too many strong hands were holding him. A few minutes later he was lying powerless on the grass, trussed up like a capon ready for broiling.

His attackers turned him on his back and lit some flares. One of the men, apparently the leader, began to search John's pockets. When he saw the letter of recommendation from Seigneur de Pontchartrain, he nodded contemptuously as if he had expected it. The contents of the saddlebags did not interest him at all, but when he opened John's valise, attached to the saddle, he and his friends could not help but show their astonishment at seeing such a large number of Louis d'Ors. Surprisingly enough, they didn't take them. The leader re-wrapped them, and put them carefully back into the valise. Turning to his men, he ordered them curtly to saddle the horse and put John on it, tied up so that he couldn't fall off. The men worked efficiently, showing that they were used to handling horses, and soon they were briskly following the leader along the post route.

John was amazed to discover that his attackers were all young. He estimated their ages to range from seventeen to slightly over twenty years old. It was not a large group. He counted only twenty-one in all. They did not say anything and when he made some remarks and asked a few questions, they pretended not to hear him. He was puzzled. At first, he thought that they were common robbers, but changed his mind quickly when he saw that they were not excited about the large amount of money he was carrying, as thieves would be. He just could not figure out who they were!

After a few miles on the post route, they turned onto a narrow trail, which they followed tirelessly for hours. A few more turns onto different trails brought them to the opening of a clearing where they were stopped by a watchman. After a venomous glance at John, he said, "I'm happy you caught that son of Belial, brothers." He then stood aside to let them pass. John did not have time to consider the remark for they walked into an open place where a young man of approximately eighteen years old, dressed as a peasant boy, was sitting on a fallen tree trunk. When he heard them, he stood up and came to them.

"How did it go, Rolland? Nobody was hurt, I hope?" he asked anxiously.

The leader of John's group stopped and said, "Praise the Lord, Jean. It was easy. We found him asleep, and before he knew what was happening we had him tied up. He has a letter of recommendation of Seigneur de Pontchartrain, our Minister of Finance, asking everybody to give him the red carpet treatment. Besides, I found fifty Louis d'Ors[51] in his valise. I put everything back again where I found it."

"Thank you, Rolland," the young man replied. "Let's question him, but first take his ropes off. I don't like him tied up. Let some of you stay close to him so that he won't try to escape."

John was even more surprised to hear these words. These men sounded like Huguenots. If that was true, they would not hurt an innocent traveler, and he felt his life was not in danger.

Jean and Rolland seated themselves on the tree and told John to stand before them. As he obeyed and walked closer to the tree the other gang members formed a circle around them. Jean, who apparently was the leader of the group, addressed John politely.

"I am Jean Cavalier, and this is Rolland.[52] Two of my men heard you talking to the innkeeper in La Mallene. You said

---

[51] Fifty Louis d'Ors correspond to approximately twenty months wages of a skilled laborer.

[52] Both men became the recognized leaders of the Huguenots in the War of the Cevennes (the War of the Camisards). Cavalier was nineteen years old when the war began. Pierre Laporte had the nickname Rolland.

Jean Cavalier

that you were heading east on the post route and showed a letter of recommendation from Seigneur de Pontchartrain, which you still have. We also found fifty Louis d'Ors in your valise. You must have obtained this large sum from the Minister of Finance, who is sending it through you to the Abbé[53] du Chaila, the arch enemy of the Church of Christ. The Abbé was killed three days ago, but we don't want you to report this to Seigneur de Bâville, the governor of Languedoc. We are Huguenots and detest men like yourself who are supporting the Roman Church, the scarlet woman of Babylon,[54] killing and torturing the followers of our Lord Jesus Christ. We intend to kill you, as you deserve, being a Judas and collaborating with the persecutors of the

---

[53] Abbé = Abbot.
[54] See Revelation 17.

Nicolas de Lamoignon de Bâville (1648-1724)

children of the church in the desert. However, we brought you here, rather than killing you in your sleep, so that you may justify yourself if you can."

"I'm not sure that I understood everything you said," John began, talking clearly and distinctly so that everybody could hear him. "I don't know the Abbé du Chaila, and I heard the name of Seigneur de Bâville for the first time in La Rochelle. One of our brothers in Christ told me that he is the one who persecutes the Church relentlessly." The faces of Jean and Rolland showed their astonishment as soon as John mentioned the words "our brothers in Christ," and the other men began to mutter to each other. John, however, acted as if he didn't hear it and continued his defense.

"I'm from Holland. My name is John Van het Woudt, and I'm here on a special mission for the Dutch government. I cannot discuss that mission in public. The Dutch government persuaded your government in Paris to give me the recommendation you mentioned so that I'm able to travel freely, and can accomplish my assignment. I'm Dutch only because I live in Holland. In reality, I'm a Huguenot who fled to Holland some years ago. I have the permission of my government to combine my assignment with a personal matter: trying to find my father, who has been serving as a galley slave in Dunkirk for years and is now being transported to Marseille. I hope and pray that I will see him shortly and can arrange for the purchase of his freedom."

"Why can't you tell us more about your mission for the Dutch government? You can trust all of us, being dedicated to Christ. We won't mention it to anyone," Rolland added, looking suspicious.

"I can't," John said simply. "I've given my word only to reveal this secret in an emergency. My life isn't an emergency, especially not because you won't take the life of your brother in Christ, which I am. I'm willing to mention somewhat more of my assignment in confidence to Mr. Cavalier or to you."

"I believe John," Cavalier said unexpectedly. "His whole attitude shows that he is telling the truth." Turning to the other men, he commanded, "All of you can go home now. I expect you all to be here again next week at the same time. Goodbye and may the Lord bless you." In an orderly way all the men except three left, after having tied John's horse Prince to one of the trees.

"Let's sit down on the grass," Jean Cavalier suggested, "It is easier to talk that way." Cavalier, Rolland, and John seated themselves and John began to explain that he was sent to bring a large amount of money to one of the leading Huguenots in Languedoc. He explained that the gift came from the king of England and from collections made by the Reformed churches in The Netherlands. The money must be given to Mr. Abraham

We are Huguenots and detest men like yourself . . .

Mazel,[55] who should use it to help the suffering members of Christ's church in Languedoc. Hearing this, Rolland cried out, "You have come to bring all that money to Abraham Mazel? We know him well. He is one of our leaders and we saw him less than a week ago!"

"John, forgive me, that I doubted your words. Now I see that you spoke the truth because you can only know Abraham Mazel's name if you are completely trusted by the Dutch or the English governments. Please, let's be friends!" added Rolland, offering his hand, which John gladly shook.

"I'm not needed here anymore, Jean," Rolland said to Cavalier. "I trust that you can direct Mr. Van het Woudt to Abraham Mazel, and help him to find his father. John, be extremely careful. Within a few days the roads may be filled with the troops of Bâville, thirsting for our blood to revenge the death of Abbé du Chaila. Goodbye, both of you. May the Lord take you both in His care!" He jumped up and walked away quickly, nearly running.

"Well, well," said Jean, smiling after the disappearing Rolland. "It seems that my friend trusts me enough to take care of you." He turned to John and went on, "I don't know what to do with you! It would be simple to let you continue your journey, but that may be dangerous because of the death of the Abbé du Chaila. Maybe it would be better if you stay with me for a few days."

"I can't afford any more delays," John said seriously. "If I can't intercept the group of convicts my father belongs to before they arrive in Marseille, my whole trip will be in vain. I must continue my travels as soon as possible. By the way, who is that Abbé du Chaila. Why will his death bring the troops of Bâville on the roads? Was he so important?"

"He was the most important person in this area," Cavalier said. "One of the three men waiting to go home with me was there when he died. Wait. I'll get him so that he can tell you himself what happened a few days ago, on July 23 and 24."

---

[55] Abraham Mazel also became one of the military leaders of the Huguenots during the War of the Cevennes.

15

THE RAID

THE three men waiting for Cavalier had disappeared from sight, but he apparently knew where they had gone. After a short time he came back with one of them, who seemed to be a peasant. Cavalier introduced him as Gérard, and requested him to tell how they had liberated the prisoners held in the basement of the house of Abbé du Chaila. Gérard seated himself comfortably opposite John on the grass, leaning his back against a fallen tree. He thought a few moments and then looked at John.

"You mentioned, John, that the Abbé du Chaila was unknown to you. That was a surprise to all of us because we thought that everyone in France had heard about him. He is the Inspector of the Mission in this diocese, which means that it is his responsibility to convert as many Huguenots to the Roman Church as possible. Besides, he is the right-hand man of our governor, Bâville, who has ordered the torturing and killing of innumerable Huguenots. The Abbé du Chaila did the same. He even had a private jail and torture room in his basement, where he began trying out a new machine which broke the bones of his victims. I really believe that such a man deserves to be killed.

"Last week Saturday,[56] Pierre Séguier, a gifted preacher, called us together for a worship service in a sheep pen high up in the mountains. It's a lonely spot and one of the few safe places left to us where the soldiers don't come. His sermon took more than two hours, which is longer than he usually preaches. He talked mainly about the Book of Judges in the Old Testament and emphasized that we must follow its outline. We must take up our arms like the judges did and fight the Wars of the Lord. We must resist the cruel attacks of the government soldiers on our wives and children, he said.

---

[56] Saturday, July 22, 1702.

"After the sermon he led us in prayer, in which he especially remembered the personal prisoners of the Abbé du Chaila. During the prayer the Holy Spirit began to speak through him and told us that we must liberate them."[57]

"You believe that the Holy Spirit was speaking through this man?" asked John incredulously, who had been taught differently.

"Of course," responded Gerard, surprised that anyone could doubt it. "We've heard it on many occasions. We often call him Pierre Esprit.[58] In fact, the Holy Spirit uses many men and women to reveal His will nowadays."

"I don't believe a word of it," John said sharply. "It is contrary to everything the Bible teaches. However, we can talk about that later. Now continue your story, please."

"Well, we know better!" Gerard said stubbornly. "Anyway, nobody wanted to resist the Holy Spirit, so all the men volunteered to help in the liberation. Pierre Esprit forbade Cavalier and two other men to go. They were too young, he said. Nevertheless, we had a large group, sixty men, some had guns and pistols, while the rest had knives and sticks.

"Pierre lined us up four men abreast, and in this way we marched to the house of Abbé du Chaila in Pont de Montvert. It took us nearly two hours to get to the bridge across the river in front of his house. We sang Psalms all the way, and sometimes Pierre reassured us that the victory would be ours because the Lord was on our side! I remember singing Psalm 68[59] while we crossed the bridge."

"I wish I had been there," Jean suddenly interrupted Gérard. "No Psalm comforts me as much as that one."

---

[57] During this period, the persecuted Church of Christ in the southern part of France also suffered from many misguided Huguenots who claimed that the Holy Spirit talked to them directly. We know, of course, that this is not true! The Holy Spirit guides us only through the Word of God, the Bible.

[58] Esprit = Spirit.

[59] The singing of this Psalm by the Huguenots became the traditional way for them to begin their battles. Its effect was incredible. A Roman Catholic officer of King Louis XIV, who was fighting against the Huguenots, remarks in a letter that as soon as the Huguenots began to sing, the officers of the Royal army could not control their troops anymore. Frequently, they panicked and fled.

To John's amazement he began to recite it with glittering eyes and after a few lines, Gérard joined in.

> *God shall arise, and by His might*
> *Put all His enemies to flight;*
> *In conquest shall He quell them.*
> *Let those who hate Him, scattered, flee*
> *Before His glorious majesty,*
> *For God Himself shall fell them.*
> *Just as the wind drives smoke away,*
> *So God will scatter the array*
> *Of those who evil cherish.*
> *As wax that melts before the fire,*
> *So, vanquished by God's dreadful ire,*
> *Shall all the wicked perish.*[60]

"Abraham Mazel, another one of our leaders," continued Gérard, "sent some of our men into the village to tell the people to stay in their houses because everyone seen outdoors would be killed. We surrounded the house of the Abbé, and were making such a noise that the whole house came alive. One of the servants opened a window, looked outside, and asked what we wanted. Brother Mazel answered that all the prisoners must be given to us in the name of God. The servant disappeared, but returned after a long time and told us that the Abbé du Chaila had ordered their release.

"We waited for hours for our brothers and sisters, but nothing happened. At last brother Mazel became so furious that he ordered us to break open the front and the back doors with axes. The Abbé must have become scared because after we had cracked open the doors, another servant brought all the prisoners outside. We all rejoiced and praised the Lord when we saw them coming. Our excitement soon changed to tears, though, for they were such a sorry sight! All of them were in pain. Some could hardly walk, others had broken arms, wrists, or worse. It was a lot of noise with all of us talking, crying, praying, kneeling, and whatever else we were doing.

---

[60] Rhymed version from the *Book of Praise* (Anglo-Genevan Psalter).

The Abbé du Chaila (1648-1702)

"At that moment, one of the ladies — yes, John, two of these martyred sisters were real ladies belonging to the nobility — began to sing Psalm 124, and we all joined in with her."[61]

> *Let Israel now say in thankfulness*
> *That if the LORD had not our right maintained*
> *And if the LORD had not with us remained*
> *When cruel man against us rose to strive,*
> *We'd surely have been swallowed up alive.*[62]

Gérard wiped his sleeve over his eyes.

"It was such a touching moment that I still get tears in my eyes when I think about it. Anyhow, after the singing, we brought our released brothers and sisters away to safer places. At that

---

[61] The suffering Church of Christ in France was a Psalm-singing church. They were singing the Psalms in prison, when they were tortured, on the galleys, and even when they were burned at the stake.

[62] Rhymed version from *Book of Praise* (Anglo-Genevan Psalter).

time we found out that Pierre Massip had not been released. He was one of the Abbé's most important prisoners because he had helped a large number of Huguenots escape from France over the years. We were still surrounding the house and several of our men went up the stairs to the door again to demand his release. Unexpectedly, one of the soldiers of Abbé du Chaila fired his gun and wounded one of them.

"We were all furious and Pierre Esprit called out that this deed must be punished by burning the house of the Abbé and everything it contained for the Lord.[63] Then most of us began to bring straw and wood from a barn close by and we piled it against the doors of the house. Brother Mazel lighted it with a burning candle and in no time at all the house was burning like a torch. In all this excitement, we had forgotten that Pierre Massip was still in jail until we suddenly heard him call for help. Thankfully his cell was in the back of the house and we were able to get him out before the flames were too hot.[64]

"Later, I heard that Abbé du Chaila had succeeded in jumping out one of the rear windows. Nobody had seen him jumping so he would have escaped if he hadn't hurt his foot. We found him close to the bridge across the river, limping along. Pierre Esprit urged him to repent of his evil deeds, to dedicate his life to Christ and to join us in living in accordance with the will of God. The Abbé du Chaila flatly refused. Pierre told him then that he deserved the death penalty for all his crimes. He admonished him again to repent and gave him time to pray to the Lord. After that, he was executed.

"For the rest of the night we continued to give thanks to the Lord and to praise His name for the wonderful escape of our brothers and sisters from the Abbé du Chaila."

"What happened to the victims of the Abbé?" asked John, who had listened spellbound.

"I understand that Pierre Massip is guiding them across the border to the Duchy of Savoy," Gérard replied.

---

[63] As in Joshua 6:17-19.

[64] The liberation of these martyrs is one of the highlights in the history of the church in France. This event, recorded here as accurately as possible, started the War of the Cevennes (1702-1710).

"Yes," said Jean Cavalier, "that is the very reason I formed this group of brothers in Christ. We are watching the roads and trying to suppress the news of the death of the Abbé du Chaila as long as possible. Every minute we gain by postponing the time that the governor will hear about it will help Pierre Massip and his group."

"I see," John admitted. "Yet, I must go as soon as possible."

He explained to Jean and Gérard where and how he intended to meet the group of convicts. He mentioned that he had no plan on how to liberate his father, but he expressed his trust that the Lord would not forsake him either and would give him the guidance he needed. Both of them listened attentively, but could not offer any suggestion that John hadn't already considered.

"In the meantime, Jean," John continued, "one of my problems can be solved easily. I'm supposed to give Abraham Mazel most of the money I carry. You seem to know him well so I'll give it to you. You can forward it to Mazel, and tell him where it comes from and for what reason. Moreover, I'm in the same predicament as your friend Massip. The sooner I leave, the less I'll be delayed by soldiers. If you agree with me, I'd like to leave now, Jean."

Jean considered John's suggestion for some time, but at last he smiled and stood up.

"I think it can be done. It sounds fine to me. However, nobody knows what will happen during the next couple of weeks. I wouldn't want you to fall into the hands of our brothers again, mistaking you for a Romanist spy. I would love to go with you, but I can't. Remember, if you are in trouble in this area you can always mention my name and I'll be happy to help you again. Besides, today I'll bring you a fair distance on your way along the post route and will show you a place where they know how to find me if it's necessary. Gérard, I will bring him to Francois Le Fevre today and I should be back by tomorrow night. Tell the others to go home, too. I'll see you then."

It was a nice experience for John to walk with Jean. The weather was fine, not too warm, with a nice breeze blowing. They guided the horse along by his halter, and every few hours they took a rest. They had many things in common, especially their worries about the Church of Christ.

During their walk, Jean asked John how he had escaped to Holland. The few times that people had asked that question, John had never told much about it. He always wondered if the people were really interested or if the question was just a matter of politeness knowing that John was a Huguenot. Now, however, he felt that Jean was genuinely interested. He told the whole story of his escape with Camille, and the liberation of his sister Manette with details that he hadn't even mentioned to his adopted father and mother.

"It's a comforting thought that the Lord leads us in different ways, but that He gives us all the opportunity to be a blessing for other people," Jean remarked thoughtfully. "You were allowed to help Camille and Manette, and the Lord gave me the opportunity to help my own father and mother."

Obviously John wanted to know what had happened to Jean's parents, and Jean didn't object to telling about it.

"My family, the Cavaliers, have always lived in the village Ribaut. My parents and all the other Huguenots in the village returned to the Roman Church when I was five or six years old. However, after a few years my father and mother repented of their betrayal of Christ and joined the Huguenots again, fully prepared to suffer for Christ if the need arose. Fortunately, the Roman priest of our village was an easygoing man so their repentance didn't have any consequences.

"I attended the Romanist school in the village, but my mother secretly taught me the Bible, the Psalms, and our creed. When I knew everything they could teach in our village school, the bishop offered me a scholarship for a Jesuit[65] college. I felt that his interest in me was dangerous so I fled to Geneva after working a short time for one of my uncles. I intended to go to Berlin where I have another uncle, but it was impossible because I didn't have any money. In Geneva I found a job in a bakery, but a short time later I received a letter from one of my friends,

---

[65] A Romanist religious order for men, founded by Ignatius Loyola in 1534, for the purpose of keeping the Roman church pure in doctrine. In non-Romanist circles, they were notorious for their fanaticism, their political influence in Romanist countries, and their easy use of the Inquisition.

who wrote that my parents had been put in prison in revenge for my fleeing abroad. I returned at once, of course, hoping to be able to free them. I wasn't even close to home when I heard that they were back again. Both had relapsed and were now New Converts.

"I came home on Sunday morning. My parents were both very glad to see me, but after a few hugs, they told me that they were just going to the Mass in the church. You can understand what that meant to me, seeing my father and mother standing with the Roman prayer book in their hands. I talked with them and admonished them to reject the papal doctrines. 'Where now are your promises that you would rather be killed than attend the Roman Mass? You made your vows in many worship services before God and man. What was their value when you now forsake your own vows?' I asked. They were listening silently, and I didn't know what they were going to do.

" 'Will I be forced in the Last Judgment to give testimony against both of you? Is it possible that you, who have been such a good example of perseverance to me, shall now destroy your brilliant future with Jesus Christ with such a devilish act?' I appealed to them. I kept talking for more than an hour, and then, at last, the Holy Spirit showed them their unfaithfulness. They repented again and now they have persevered. A few months ago they were imprisoned anew in Alais. I can't reach them, but it's a great comfort to know that they are willing to persevere in the faith of Jesus Christ."[66]

John didn't know what to say after he had listened to this sad story. He admired his friend for his faith, and was glad that he didn't have to comfort him.

Finally, they reached the farm of Francois Le Fevre, where John was properly introduced to the farmer and his wife. Jean explained to Francois who John was and emphasized that he must be warned directly if Francois received a call for help from John. After saying this, he said goodbye to John and left.

---

[66] This is the true biography of Jean Cavalier. He was the 19-year-old general of the Huguenots during the War of the Cevennes, when they rebelled against the massacres of their brothers and sisters in Christ by the French government.

Jean's mother passed away the following year. His father was still imprisoned several years later.

126

16

A STUNNING TRANSFORMATION

IT had been raining all day long, not a heavy downpour, but a continuous drizzle. Late in the afternoon it stopped, but John, seeing the overcast sky, decided that sleeping in the open field would be even more uncomfortable than riding a horse in the rain in daytime. This night would be one of the times that he would stay at an inn, he decided. The thought of drying himself before a good fire, eating a decent meal and sleeping in a dry bed perked him up a good deal. The last two days he had been following the post route, which his father and the other convicts had most likely followed. He might meet them anytime now, he assured himself.

For the last half hour he had seen the steeple of a church tower ahead of him, so he knew he was close to a town. He was getting used to riding every day until sundown, but today he felt so wet and soppy that even though it was only mid-afternoon, he would stay in that town if there was a good inn.

The town seemed to be fairly small. It did not have walls and gates. Simple houses had been built on either side of the post route and side streets branched off with more houses. While he rode past the first few of them, he wondered why it was so quiet. No one was on the street, not even children.

Well, it looks like everybody has gone away, he thought. Maybe they are having a meeting at the town hall. I wouldn't be surprised if they have heard about the death of the Abbé du Chaila and are taking action to prevent the revolt of the Huguenots in their town.

He did not see any house that was empty or ransacked, which was a sure sign that very few, if any, Huguenots had lived in this town.

It must be a very Romanist town, he thought contemptuously, when for the third time he saw a shrine in one of the streets aligned with a large crucifix and images of saints.

While riding slowly through the street he continuously heard a low noise as if all the bees in a beehouse were excited and ready for a sting attack. It became louder when he approached the town center where the market place was, as he could see from afar. A large crowd had gathered, many of them swearing and cursing and making mocking or menacing gestures to something in the center of the square. When he reached the outskirts of the crowd, he could see over the people's heads three soldiers on horseback. They seemed to be either standing or slowly moving around somewhere in the center of the crowd. When he saw them, he suddenly realized that he most likely had achieved the purpose of his trip: he had reached the group of convicts his father was traveling with!

He had so often thought of meeting his father and how he should behave without betraying himself that he remained quite calm. Obviously, he wanted to see his father as soon as possible, but all the people in front of him formed a living wall, obstructing his way.

I've at least got the advantage of sitting on a horse who can do the pushing for me, he thought, looking with disgust at the people moving around. It will be easy to worm my way through to the soldiers. How mistaken he was! He steered his horse into the crowd, forcing his way in more and more without paying any attention to the angry looks and words of the people whom he pushed aside so relentlessly. The first few yards he made quite some progress because the people tried to back away from his horse. But then his horse happened to push his head against a short, broad-shouldered man, who instantly turned around and grasped the horse at his bridle.

"Who do you think you are, trying to push me?" he yelled furiously. "You aren't wanted here, stranger! Go back to where you came from or I'll throttle you with my own hands!" At the same time he hit the horse cruelly on the nose, and yelled, "Backwards, I say," forcing him back, encouraged by the people around him who made fun of the situation. In a few minutes John was forced out of the crowd and pushed against the wall of a stone church building.

Before the man could do more, the doors of the church were thrown wide open, and the priest with some choir boys and acolytes, wearing crucifixes, appeared. The crowd respectfully drew back so that the little procession could walk toward the market center. This helped John. The people, pushing against each other to make a path for the priest, forced the man holding the bridle against the wall, too. With a sudden swing of his head, the horse neighed loudly and rubbed the man's hand against the rough bricks. The man, with a subdued cry of pain, had to release his grip. John saw it. Instinctively, he put his heels in the sides of the horse, and let him jump into the gap between the acolytes and the crowd. Once he was there, he succeeded in keeping his horse just behind the last acolyte of the procession, which moved slowly to the town center. He heard the man yell a few curses, but the people pressed forward so that the man could not reach him anymore.

The first thing John saw in the center of the market square was a large group of convicts, most of them sitting on the ground, surrounded by foot soldiers under the control of three officers on horseback. They saluted the priest politely and in return the priest gave them a nonchalant blessing with two of his fingers. He did not stop, but continued to another group of heavily shackled[67] men with metal collars, all connected to the same chain. They were accompanied by several women and by some small children.

This group was mainly surrounded by town women and children, shouting and swearing. When they saw the priest they

---

[67] The weight of the shackles was sometimes fifty pounds.

stopped their cursing, probably expecting his approval, and watched him until he was close to the prisoners.

There he halted, indicated with his hands for his followers to stand behind him, and began to admonish the small group of convicts in a loud voice. He addressed them as cursed Huguenots who would go to hell if they wouldn't repent. The gist of his speech was that the Roman Catholic Church, their Mother, would forgive their sins if they were sorry for their evil deeds and repented. He, as one of its representatives, would personally make sure that they would be released tonight if they would return to the church. He ended his speech with the words, "We, in this town, will take care of your tired feet, dress your wounds, and I, your priest, can assure you that our governor will pay you enough to live well the rest of your life." Although he apparently expected some reaction from the Huguenots, none of them even showed that they had listened. The priest, after waiting a few minutes, became furious.

"Now I see again that you are stubborn, wicked heretics. I can do nothing for you if you don't repent! Don't complain if the people of this town punish you for your evil attitudes," he warned. He then turned away from the group and disappeared with his followers into the crowd.

In the meantime, John had scrutinized the Huguenots closely. There were about fourteen men, several women, and a few children. His father was standing somewhat behind an old man with white hair, who was surrounded by three young men and two women with children in their arms. He looked thinner and shorter than he remembered from his youth. His back was slightly bent, and he had a long, black beard. His face was grim while he watched the crowd.

After the priest with his followers had gone, the town women became very offensive.[68] Their leader was a heavy-set hag with

---

[68] The following episode is a true story and is well documented. The old man with the white hair was the father of three famous sons, who were with him when this event happened. Their family name was Hubert, and the sons were nicknamed Hubert of the Birds, Hubert of the Ants, and Hubert of the Bees because of their knowledge about birds and insects.

a shrill, loud voice. She began to revile the Huguenots again and to dance in front of them shaking her fists. This did not seem to satisfy her, for suddenly she stopped, bent down, grabbed some mud from the street, and slung it in the face of one of the Huguenot men. The other women followed her example, and in a very short time, all of them, including their children, began to throw mud at the faces of the Huguenots. Soon the small Huguenot children began to cry, holding their mud-smeared hands and arms before their eyes.

At that moment, John heard the old man with the white hair tell the Huguenots to fall on their knees and to call upon the Lord. He led them in prayer with a loud, bright voice that could be heard clearly and the others joined him. "Gracious God, who seest the wrongs to which we are hourly exposed, give us strength to bear them, and to forgive in charity those who wrong us. Strengthen us from good even unto better. Amen."

Astonished, the women and children stopped their yelling, and apparently embarrassed, dropped their mud balls on the ground. After the prayer, one of the Huguenots began to sing Psalm 116, and after the first words, the whole group sang with him.

I love the LORD, the fount of life and grace;
He heard my voice, my cry and supplication,
Inclined His ear, gave strength and consolation;
In life, in death, my heart will seek His face.

The cords of death held me in deep despair;
The terrors of the grave caused me to languish.
I suffered untold grief and bitter anguish;
In my distress, I turned to God in prayer.

In all His people's presence I will pay
My vows to Him, the LORD so good and gracious.
To God the death of all His saints is precious;
In times of grief He is their help and stay.

*I am, O L*ORD*, Thy servant, bound yet free,*
Thy handmaid's son, whose shackles Thou hast broken.
Redeemed by grace, I'll render as a token
Of gratitude my constant praise to Thee.[69]

Everyone in the market place, even the convicted criminals and the soldiers, listened silently, impressed by the unexpected attitude of the Huguenots. They had expected complaints and outcries, but heard words of trust in God.

The sudden silence was broken by the voice of the leading woman who, with tears rolling down her face, called to her cronies.

"Stop it, girls. These aren't criminals as we were told! They are better, godfearing people than we are. Why did I ever believe the stories that they are criminals, murderers, and thieves, enemies of every decent woman. Criminals can't pray and sing like these suffering people." Suddenly she went to the white haired man and fell on her knees before him.

"Oh, Father, we have sinned. We should have helped you and we made you suffer more. Forgive us. We didn't know you are a godfearing people. Have pity on us." The old man grabbed her hand.

"Stand up, my sister," he said. "Don't kneel for me but kneel for the Lord God and ask His forgiveness. We forgive you with all our hearts, and I'm sure that our Father in heaven will forgive you also, as you repent from your sins."

"Thank you, Father," the woman said, and her face brightened with thankfulness. She stood up and seeing that several other women also wept, she addressed them with a voice filled with emotion.

"Girls, this good man told me that they have forgiven us and that the good Lord has forgiven us also. I believe him because he has shown to be a good, Christian man. Therefore, don't cry anymore, but let's help reduce their suffering. Please, bring

---

[69] Psalm 116:1, 2, 8, 9 from the *Book of Praise* (Anglo-Genevan Psalter). The Huguenots probably sang the whole Psalm.

water and linen so that we can wash the mud from their faces. Hurry, girls. In the meantime, I'll see the commanding officer and will ask his permission to give these godfearing people shelter in our barn tonight." She had barely finished talking when the women were already busy, some of them went away to fetch water and linen, others helped the convicts, especially the Huguenot women, to sit down and make themselves as comfortable as they could under the circumstances. Their leader hurried away to the commanding officer.

John had heard and seen everything with mixed feelings. At the beginning he had difficulty restraining himself, but later he was very much impressed by the Christian attitude of the Huguenots and was comforted by their prayer and singing. He had already made up his mind that he shouldn't make himself known to his father while they were surrounded by so many people. It would be too dangerous. Therefore, he turned his horse and slowly rode back, intending to find a decent sleeping place and to return after dark. The people silently made room for him, wondering who he was.

When he was close to the commanding officer, he saw him listening to the leading woman. After she stopped talking, he shook his head several times. John understood that the officer refused to give his permission. He realized at once that he might help her with his excellent credentials and rode to the officer, interrupting the woman's renewed pleas by politely taking off his hat to him.

"Sir, my name is John Van het Woudt. I'm here with a special assignment from the king. I heard the petition of this woman and think that you should give her the desired permission." The officer did not hide his amazement that a civilian dared to address him, an officer of the king, and give advice in a matter that wasn't his business.

"Please, Sir," he said, haughtily but politely, "show me your papers to prove that you have the authority to interfere."

John took the letter of recommendation from his breast pocket and handed it to the officer, who took the time to read it thoroughly.

"Yes, Sir," the officer said. "I see that you have the right to ask for my protection, but I don't see that you have the right to give undesired advice. Even so, these Huguenots are the most dangerous people in our kingdom, far more than the common criminals, and I don't see why they should be given privileged treatment. I maintain that all the convicts must be given the same shelter and that no exceptions can be made."

"Sir," John replied, "my recommendation mentions specifically that I have the assignment and the right to interrogate Huguenot prisoners, and that you must give me any help needed. I'm not going to question them surrounded by all kinds of common criminals. Therefore, I request politely that you will help me in my assignment by granting the permission this woman is asking."

The officer, who did not know if John had enough authority to discredit him at the governor's headquarters, felt it better to give in on such an unimportant issue. He turned to John and asked how long the interviews would last. John indicated that he might be able to complete them in one night, whereupon the officer turned to the woman and said curtly, "Permission granted. Four of my soldiers will accompany the heretics. You better make sure that they are at the marketplace by seven o'clock tomorrow morning. For every Huguenot missing, we will burn down two houses in town." Then he lifted his hat to John, turned his horse, and rode away.

John turned to the woman and said haughtily, in his role as a government official, "Good woman, tell me where your barn is so that I can question the heretics tonight."

"This is a dead end street," she said obediently, indicating with her finger a small road at the left side of the church, "My farm is at the very end of it. The barn where the Huguenots will sleep is at the right side of the road, Sir."

"I expect to be at your place this evening after supper," John replied. "I want you to wait for me on the road with somebody to hold my horse when I'm with the prisoners. Wait," he added when the woman began to walk back to the Huguenots. "Is there a good inn in this town?"

"Yes, Sir. The inn is across from the church." The woman pointed in the proper direction. "And a good inn it is, Sir. Well known in the area!"

With a nod of his head, John dismissed the woman and slowly rode across the square. He noted that the people treated him respectfully, probably because they had heard his conversation with the leading officer, he thought.

Now that the excitement had lessened somewhat, he felt again how wet his clothes were. A good meal and an opportunity to dry himself would be welcome. He did not need a room at the inn for that night. If he could free his father, as he hoped, they must leave the city as soon as possible and go into hiding. If he failed, he didn't need a room either, he considered grimly. They would treat him as a Huguenot and chain him to the party of Huguenots. Yet he decided to take a room. It would make him less suspicious if it was thought that he was staying overnight.

17

JOHN MAKES A DECISION

AFTER enjoying a simple supper, John left the inn around eight o'clock to see his father. He had told the innkeeper that he would most likely return late at night. Nobody needed to stay up for him as long as he knew where to find the stable boy. He could then wake him up to take care of his horse. The innkeeper showed John the stable (the boy slept inside, next to the door on some straw), and told him that he would leave a lit candle on the table close to the back door of the inn so that John could easily find the way back to his room.

It was not dark yet when John saw the barn where the Huguenots were sheltered. The woman and a tall boy were waiting for him in front of the barn at the end of the street. John jumped off of his horse and gave the reins to the boy who then began to walk away with the animal toward a rundown stable across the field behind the barn.

"Wait," John said. "It's not necessary to stable the horse. I don't think my interrogation will last more than a few hours. You can hold on to the horse here. Let him eat some grass on the side of the street, but don't go too far away. I don't want to look for you in the dark after I'm finished questioning the heretics.

"Please ask the officer supervising the four soldiers to come here," John addressed the woman. "I want to talk with him."

"Sir, he won't listen to a simple woman like me," she objected, hesitating.

"Tell the officer that I'm ordering him to come and that he better obey immediately if he knows what is good for him," John retorted, as if he were a high-ranking official.

136

After waiting several minutes, John saw one of the soldiers coming to him. "I'm in charge of the soldiers assigned to watch these religious convicts, Sir," the man said politely.

"You know who I am, right?" said John, "I have the duty and permission to interrogate the prisoners. Therefore, I want the women and children on one side of the barn, supervised by two of your men.

"The male Huguenots must stay on the other side. The watchmen must be far enough away so that the prisoners understand that their responses are kept confidential. Mind you, I know your methods, but I don't accept abuse of the prisoners when you are separating them. You hear me, don't you?" John emphasized loudly, his face close to the face of the soldier. "No abuses at all! The town women may help you separate them! Also light a few candles so that I can distinguish the faces of the prisoners. Warn me as soon as they're ready!"

The moving of the prisoners went quite smoothly, apparently, because very soon the same soldier came back to John and reported politely that his orders had been carried out.

"All right," John said authoritatively, "Bring me to the prisoners."

It was quiet when John entered the barn. He saw with satisfaction that the town women had taken excellent care of the Huguenots. Also, his orders had been carried out. The soldiers and some town women were sitting close to the only entrance of the barn. The Huguenot women and their children were mostly asleep lying on old mattresses at one side of the barn. The men, on the other side, were sitting quietly on a clean layer of straw, talking softly to each other. They did not show the slightest interest in John walking slowly toward them, probably expecting another attempt to convert them. When he was close, they stopped talking and remained sitting with downcast eyes. John had not expected this, but it made it much easier for him. He remained standing in front of them, and began in a low voice to say the few sentences he had prepared beforehand.

"Brothers, I have come to bring a surprise to one of you." He saw that some of them glanced up quickly, amazed that he used the word "brothers." "It is dangerous for me if you show any emotion when I reveal the surprise. For the moment you have to believe me. Please, control yourselves when I tell you who I am."

He saw his father looking at the ground in front of him without paying any attention to his words.

"I am the son of one of you. My name is John." Suddenly, his father looked up and a flash of recognition crossed his face.

"Dad, don't show that you recognize me," John warned rapidly, looking at his father. He saw his father's eyes fill with tears and his lips tremble. A happy smile appeared on his face, but suddenly it changed. A suspicious glance came in his eyes. The smile disappeared and was replaced by a harsh look.

"Oh, Lord, don't punish me with a son who has become a New Convert," he groaned. John, understanding that his father suspected him of having purchased his freedom by joining the Roman church, also felt his eyes fill with tears.

"No, Dad, I'm not a New Convert," he stated emphatically, "I've not denied our faith. I haven't compromised. Please, believe me! Don't expect me to be a traitor of our Lord."

The white-haired old man suddenly came to his rescue.

"Brother l'Ardeur," he said to John's father. "I believe your son. Be happy that he is here and give thanks to the Lord that he was able to come."

Hearing this, John's father brightened up again. He smiled, and asked in a low voice how John's mother and sister Manette were doing.

"Mother went to be with the Lord three years after you were sent to the galleys. Manette and I fled to Holland. Manette is now living in the house of one of our Huguenot ministers, who also fled to Holland. We've tried to find you all these years so that we could help you, but nobody knew where you were. I was sent to France by the Dutch government and have used this opportunity to search for you. In Dunkerque I talked with Jean Marteilhe who told me your new name and where you might be. I thank the Lord that at last I've found you.

"Please, all of you, stay where you are and pretend that I'm trying to convert you. I got permission from the French government to interrogate Huguenots and to offer them freedom if they were willing to teach Romanists their knowledge of cloth and paper manufacturing. That offer is nothing but a mean fake. They want to get all the information they can from you and then will kill you. I use this assignment as a pretense for talking to our brothers and sisters in Christ and sometimes helping them. However, it's of the utmost importance that I keep my true identity secret, and for that reason you must not show any emotion that can give me away. It is awkward to talk to you like that, I know, but it can't be helped."

They talked for a long time. At last, John felt that he must leave so that the people wouldn't become suspicious.

"Dad, we must stop talking now," he said. "At this moment, I can't do much for all of you, but I think I can get you out, Dad. It won't be easy, but a bribe for one or two of the soldiers may work. If I don't succeed tonight, I'll try again tomorrow. What do you think about it?"

His father was silent for several minutes. At last he asked John where he had gotten the money and John explained that it was from the Dutch government to be used for the Huguenots. His next question was, "Can't you purchase all our lives?"

"Dad, I don't think you understand. I don't have enough money to purchase your freedom. Your liberation can only be done by either kidnaping you, which is very difficult, or by bribing. I'm extremely sorry that I can't do anything for the others, but I promise faithfully that I'll ask the Dutch government to take care of the others when I'm back in Holland." Hearing this, some of the Huguenots asked a few more questions about the Huguenots in Holland, which John answered as well as he could while his father considered his suggestion. At last, everybody stopped talking, waiting for John's father to respond to his son's offer.

Finally he lifted his head up and looked John straight in his face.

"I'm thankful to the Lord that He has given me the favor of seeing you and hearing that you and Manette are godfearing children. I would love to accept your offer and go with you, but it's impossible. I can't accept it. If I would escape with your help, the others will be punished cruelly. I can't take that responsibility. I would rather keep suffering for Christ than increase the suffering of these brothers and sisters in Christ. I don't want to talk about it anymore. John, I understand how difficult it already is for you to go and leave me behind. However, it isn't as hard for me as it has been all these past years. I've seen you now and heard about Manette after all these years. This will be a good comfort for the rest of my life on this earth. Please, take good care of my little one, Manette. May the Lord keep you both in His care. And now, please go." He let his tears stream freely along his cheeks, and did a brave but vain effort to compose himself. The old man whispered comforting words to him, at the same time gesturing to John that he must leave.

John swallowed a few times, clamped his teeth together, and managed to give his face a severe look. He stood up, and after a last, long look at his father, he turned, went to the barn entrance and left. The boy was still at the same spot, holding his horse. John, too upset to talk, took the reins, mounted and steered the horse towards the inn.

After he had gone a short distance, he suddenly straightened his back.

"What a fool I am," he muttered to himself. "Dad doesn't want to be liberated in a way that endangers the others? Well, I'm not going to let him down. I'll certainly try to free them all, the Lord willing. Jean Cavalier must help. It's a long ride in the dark to get him, but I'll make it one way or the other.

"It will be a tiresome night for you, Prince. You'll have to keep running with few breaks for rest. Please, do your best," he addressed his horse. "Let's go!" Resolutely, he cantered the horse through town and took the road to Alais where his new Huguenot friends knew how to reach Jean Cavalier.

18

THE GORGE

A very tired horse walked slowly to the door of a small farmhouse deep in the hills of Mons, not far from Alais, just as the sun peeked over the eastern horizon. Its rider, John, dismounted slowly, feeling stiff and aching all over from riding all night without stopping. After throwing the reins over one of the poles of an enclosure in which a pig was lazily enjoying the coolness of the mud, he went through the open door into the house. Francois, the farmer, was sitting at the table with a small girl on his lap. His wife was busy at the stove and two small boys, lying on a straw mattress on the floor, were just waking up.

When John entered, it was still too dark in the room to distinguish the surprised faces of the farmer and his wife. He only saw two shadowy persons, but was so happy to have arrived that he completely forgot to ascertain that they were the friends of Jean.

"I'm sorry I didn't knock, but I'm in a hurry." he said bluntly. "I want to see Jean. Jean Cavalier. Do you know where he is?"

The farmer put the little girl on the floor and stood up. He did not recognize John either, but was more careful in not committing himself.

"Jean Cavalier? He isn't here, Sir. Why do you ask me? He doesn't live in this area at all. What a pity that you were sent to the wrong house. Have you come a long way? You must be tired. Please, sit down on my chair and rest a while, Sir." When John went to the chair, the woman suddenly recognized him.

"Oh, is it you, John? We thought that you had gone to your own country. Be welcome, young man. Wouldn't you like something to eat or to drink?"

Without waiting for an answer, she took a pitcher that stood on the table and poured some milk in a mug and gave it to him. John drank it and repeated his question.

"Where is Jean, Francois? I need him most urgently."

"I'm happy to see you again, John," the farmer said heartily. Anxious to help him as he had promised Jean Cavalier, he added, "He isn't here. However, I know where to find him, but you look so tired that I don't think you can go with me. I've got to go along some steep mountain roads. How urgently do you really need him?"

John, feeling so tired that he could barely stay awake, looked him directly in his face, and said, speaking slowly, "Francois, my father and a group of other brothers in Christ are being transported to Marseille, to the galleys. We can liberate them if we don't delay. I rode the whole night to ask for Jean's help and to tell him where they are. Three times I lost my way in the dark, but I made it. You are right. I can't go with you because I'm dead tired and need some rest. So does my horse. Maybe you can go to Jean and give him the message that I have returned and need him badly."

The farmer scratched his head a few times and looked at his wife.

"What do you think, Mother? Let's put that young man in the haystack so that he can sleep. His horse goes to the barn, and I will be on my way to Jean. Isn't that the best thing to do?" The woman agreed with a nod of her head. She insisted that John should first eat some breakfast before going to sleep.

"John, it'll take most of the day to find Jean. I won't be back before late in the afternoon. Therefore, take your time and sleep. I'll wake you up when I've come back."

*   *   *

"I hope you're feeling all right again, John," he heard someone say. He opened his eyes, and saw his friend, Jean Cavalier, standing in the hay at his feet. He jumped up and greeted his friend with a hug and a smile.

"Oh Jean, how happy I am to see you. I found my father but he refused to leave the other Huguenots in his group. He said that we must liberate all or none, and I came to you for help. You and your men can liberate them, I'm sure."

"Well, John, it's good to see you again. Francois gave me your message and I sent messengers to all my friends to meet me here. As a matter of fact, some have already arrived. While we wait for the others you must tell me what happened. Where and when did you find your father? How large is the group of convicts, and how many of them are our brothers in Christ? How many soldiers are guarding them?" He sat down in the straw and listened quietly while John related all the events of the previous day. Once in a while he interrupted John to clarify some detail.

"I think that we can free these poor people, John," Jean said thoughtfully, after John had finished his story. "They have to go through a gorge, south of the village of Coudelet, if I understand you correctly. That is the very place to trap them, but it is far away. We have a lot of walking to do to be there in time. Can you make it, do you think? How are you feeling, John? Rested?"

"I'm not as fit as I'd like to be, but I can make it. Don't worry," John said with a crooked smile. "After all, I still have my horse, right?"

"All right, then, let's go to the others and explain our plans," Jean suggested, standing up and going down the haystack with John following.

Approximately twenty young men were standing in front of the barn. Francois appeared to be the oldest, and he was not even thirty years old. John did not recognize all of them, but they all seemed to know John and he heard many friendly greetings. They gathered around Jean anxious to hear his instructions. He explained shortly why he had called them and explained his plans for liberating John's father and the other martyrs.

"I'm happy that we are in good shape and love to walk," he added teasingly. "We've got to keep going the whole night and part of tomorrow morning so that the group won't escape us. I know that some of you may not be able to do it. Everyone who is afraid that he can't make it may go home."

Thankfully, John noticed that everybody stayed and that not even the youngest boys, who were barely fourteen years old,[70] were willing to leave. Next, Jean asked them to take along as many heavy rods as possible, as well as a good supply of chisels, files, and hammers for removing the shackles from the Huguenots.

When they left half an hour later, Francois brought John's horse to him, expecting him to ride instead of walk. John felt embarrassed about getting this special treatment and suggested that the weaker ones of the group should take turns in riding, each for half an hour.

They were all tired when they reached the gorge in the afternoon of the following day. Everyone sat down in the grass and Jean again explained his plan of attack.[71] He wanted to barricade the southern part of the gorge with heavy rocks, and as soon as the convict group had entered the chasm, some of Jean's men must loosen heavy rocks, let them fall behind them and close the gap. If that worked, the whole group would be in their power and they could negotiate for the release of the Huguenot convicts.

*   *   *

Sieur du Moulin, the commanding officer, riding ahead of the group of convicts, was in a bad mood. He was bored with the regular routine of his assignment, which had lasted for several weeks and would take at least another week before they reached their final destination, Marseille. It was bad enough to guide a

---

[70] It was not uncommon that young boys of twelve and thirteen years old fought with their father against the suppressors.

[71] This plan is typical for the Huguenot battles during these times. They were able to take advantage of the country layout, which they knew far better than the Royal troops.

144

hundred convicts along with the help of no more than a score of soldiers and two officers reporting to him, but the news of the death of the Abbé du Chaila made it even worse. Last night he had heard that Bâville had sent special troops to capture the rebels. He was greatly disappointed about not being able to join these special troops. That would have been fun, but instead he was burdened with this dull assignment. Was there anything more monotonous than the scheme he himself had designed — ten minutes rest after every hour walking?

Deep in thought, he paid little attention to the road, which led through a chasm as it had so often before. The ravine made a sharp angle, and when he went around the bend, he halted in surprise. A very large rock, at least eight feet high, was barricading the road, leaving only a small opening on one side where a young man was standing.

"You can't pass through here, Sir," the young man said distinctly. Sieur du Moulin halted, astonished that a common peasant boy dared to address him without permission. One of his officers and the five soldiers following him also stared in surprise at that insignificant-looking young man. At the same time, they heard a noise as if a large rock was sliding along the mountain, ending with a loud thud on the road. "That rock closes the road behind you, Sir," the young man said composedly. "My name is Jean Cavalier, and I suggest that you and I sit down together to discuss your problem of leaving the trap you have walked into."

Without answering, Sieur du Moulin grasped his sword and unsheathed it, intending to slay Jean. Just as he dug his spurs into the horse's side for a deadly charge, a large boulder came whizzing through the air and slammed into the ground in front of the horse. The horse reared high and would have bolted, but Sieur du Moulin, an experienced horse rider, dropped his sword, grabbed the reins with both hands and managed to regain control of the horse. While he calmed the horse down, he glanced up to see who had thrown the rock. Both sides of the glen were occupied by men who looked like farmers. They were

A large boulder came whizzing through the air and slammed into the ground in front of the horse.

sitting or standing in relaxed attitudes, but in front of them were piles of rocks, ready to be hurled down. A few men close to the commander were using iron bars to disengage another big boulder.

"Well, Seigneur, don't you think it's better to sit down and discuss the terms of your surrender?" Jean's voice had a threatening note in it. "Maybe you haven't noticed, but four of my men are keeping you covered with their guns. I ordered them to kill you if you make a wrong move. I don't think I've got enough patience to wait any longer. I'll count to three and if you haven't dismounted your horse you'll die. One, two . . ." Before he could say three, the Sieur du Moulin had jumped to the ground and given the reins to one of the officers following him. He told them to stop the group and went to Jean. When he was approximately ten feet away, Jean ordered him to wait. Two of Jean's friends appeared from behind the large boulder. Together with Jean, they walked a little closer to Sieur du Moulin. They sat down on the road close to him and told him to come and do the same.

"We want you to surrender now," Jean said curtly. "Our terms are simple. You give us all the Huguenot convicts and all your firearms. Four of your soldiers must help to remove their chains. As soon as they are all free, we'll bring them to a safe place while some of us will remain here to cover our retreat. When all my men have withdrawn, you're free to continue your journey. Do you agree with the terms?"

"How much time are you giving me to consider your proposal?" the commanding officer asked haughtily, embarrassed that he must negotiate with a peasant boy.

"No time at all! You've got to give me your answer now. If not, I'll order my men to stone all of you. In fact, it seems to me that my men, supported by the convicts, can liquidate you and your men completely."

"You mentioned the other convicts. You want them too?"

"No! They are murderers, thieves, pickpockets, and other kinds of criminals. They are undergoing deserved punishment for their felonies while the Huguenots are innocent of any crime. We are only concerned about our brothers and sisters, the Huguenots," Jean replied.

"A last question. What about eating and drinking? We can't survive without water and food," the officer stated, trying to buy time while he thought of a way out.

"We will provide you with enough water and with some food. I'm sure it won't be enough, but we haven't got much ourselves. Don't worry, nobody has ever died by fasting one or two days. Well, do you accept the terms?"

"I surrender and accept the terms, provided we are allowed to keep our swords."

"You may. If you pledge to me on your word of honor as an officer in the Royal army that you'll faithfully adhere to our terms, we'll let you walk freely in this gorge. If you don't give your word of honor, we'll keep you hostage on this spot, watched by four of my men," Jean said.

"All right, I give my word of honor," Sieur du Moulin pledged. "I will order my two officers to discuss the details of the release of the Huguenots with you and your people." He stood up, hesitated a moment, and then called his officers to inform them of his decision.

John had kept himself in the background during the negotiations because he and Jean thought it better not to make the officers or soldiers aware of the role John had played.

When the officers talked to Jean, they expressed their concern that all the other convicts could revolt when they saw the release of the Huguenots. After some discussion, Jean and Francois agreed that the Huguenots should be removed from the other convicts without drawing their attention. A few of the soldiers then went to the Huguenots, told them they were needed in front of the column, and guided them all, men, women, and children, past the other convicts. They did not give them any special attention, being unaware of the attack. When they passed through the opening next to the big boulder in front they saw John and Jean's men waiting for them and were told they were free.

First, they barely believed it, afraid that it was another trick of their persecutors, but when John went to his father and hugged him, all doubts were removed. Then everyone became excited, hugging, kissing, and laughing, until the old man fell on his knees and with a loud, glad voice called on them to praise the Lord. He led them in prayer as he had done so often before, but this time he thanked the Lord God with words of joy, loaded with exaltation.

The Huguenots and the four soldiers worked diligently to remove the shackles. When this was finally completed, most of the Huguenots, especially the women and children stretched themselves on the grass for their first night's sleep as free people.

Jean sat down with Francois, the old man, and John's father to discuss their plans. All agreed that an effort should be made to bring all the Huguenots across the border.

"Some of us can't go that far, brothers," the old man warned, "They have sores because of the shackles, and most of the women are exhausted. We need some time to recover before we can start moving toward the border."

"We expected that," Jean replied with a smile. "We have hiding places, high up in the mountains where the soldiers will never find you. We plan to bring you there during the next few days. When all of you are in good health again, Pierre Massip, a guide, will bring you across the border to Switzerland, the Lord willing. No, that isn't a problem. Our difficulty is that we don't know what to do with you, John. What are your plans?"

"Well, I'm not sure where to go from here," John said thoughtfully. "My assignment was to go to Dunkerque. There I was supposed to find a ship going to Genoa and travel by road to Savoy. I can't go to Genoa for the simple reason that I feel it's too dangerous to go to Marseille with my father. Somebody might recognize him, or me for that matter, and then we'll be in trouble. We've got to go over land, which isn't too hard for me alone, having good credentials. The difficulty is that I don't know how to take my father with me. If caught without a passport, he may lose his life. We can't risk that. Do you have any suggestions?"

"I don't want to be a burden to you, John. It's quite simple. I'll go with the other Huguenots. I understand that we will be in Switzerland within a few weeks and there you can contact me to go to Holland," John's father suggested quietly.

"No, Dad, I disagree," John objected. "I don't want to be separated from you again. I've waited long enough for your delivery and now you must go with me to Holland. Don't you worry, I'll find a way."

"You must still be sleepy, John, that you don't see how easy it is," teased Jean, with an amused grin at his joke. "Up till now you've played the role of an official on a royal assignment quite well, but you're not as convincing as you could be. An official never travels alone. They always have a servant, and that is the perfect role for your father. I'm sure that nobody would dare to ask for the papers of the man who is serving you, a highly respected envoy of the king!"

Dumbfounded, John listened to his friend's proposal. He turned it over in his mind, and saw its great merits.

"I think your idea is marvelous," he praised his friend. "A few things must be solved, though. My father must be decently dressed and he needs to ride. I've still got enough money to purchase things. Where can we buy some clothes for him, and a mule, which would be the best animal for a servant. Cheap and strong."

"I suggest that Francois takes you home again, and that either he or you both go to Alais to buy these things," Jean suggested. After everybody agreed, the party broke up and they stretched their tired bodies on the grass to get a few more hours of sleep before a day with new problems would set in.

19

HUGUENOT REFUGEES

THE forest was quiet as the end of the night approached. In another hour the sun would creep above the horizon and the daily routine of finding food while on guard against all enemies would begin for most forest animals. Even tame animals were completely at rest at this time of the night. John's horse, Prince, was lying on the ground and his father's mule was standing several yards away, both tied to a tree. Between the two animals the riders slept peacefully, knowing that the horses would become restless if anyone approached them.

They had traveled several days along the post route except when the road went through a village or a small city. It was safer to avoid them, which they had done by leaving the main road temporarily, and using country roads and by-paths to circumvent these communities. They did not mind that their progress was very slow and that they never encountered an inn or any other lodging. Sleeping in the open during this time of the year was far more agreeable than staying in expensive, hot, and often dirty, inns. Even food was no problem. It was much cheaper to purchase their food from the few farms they passed than to eat in regular eating places.

John's father had recovered fast from his ordeal as a galley slave. It was an agreeable surprise when he discovered that his arms and legs had become uncommonly strong as a result of his daily rowing in spite of his poor diet.

Their progress to the border of France was slow. They rode carefully without talking, all their attention directed to the road ahead of them in the hope of hearing or seeing the patrolling soldiers before they were seen themselves. Three times it had worked. The soldiers were so noisy that John and his father had enough time to hide, once behind a barn, once behind some bushes and the third time behind a large pile of rocks in a field.

Their days had a uniform pattern. At daybreak they began their journey, halting only two times daily for a short rest. During the mid-afternoon they began to look for a safe camping place, stopped when they found one, and prepared for the night. There was so much to talk about after all those years they had not seen each other that sitting together during the rest of the afternoon and the evening was quite a treat for both of them.

Yesterday, the road, which for days had gone through rather open country with low hills of rocks, began to wind its way through a forest. Their selected sleeping place was farther away from the road than on previous nights. Both were well acquainted with forests and inadvertently had penetrated deeper into it because of the sheer pleasure of walking under the trees and smelling its woody odor.

John's father, who had been sleeping as if he had to make up for all the sleepless nights aboard the galley, suddenly woke up. Did he imagine it or was it true that he had heard a baby? He sat up and rubbed his eyes. Yes, there it was again, a barely audible sound of a tiny baby crying. For a few moments he remained in his sitting position wondering what the sound really was. In all his experience he had never heard such a sound in the forest. The crying became gradually more audible as if the baby became impatient because nobody gave it any attention. Resolutely, John's father crept to John, pushed him softly, and whispered, "John, wake up. It sounds as if a baby is crying. Do you know what it can be?"

John awoke with a start, and then sat up and listened.

"How long has that been going on, Dad?" he whispered.

"I don't know, I just woke up," his father replied. "Don't you think that we should find out what it means? Maybe we are needed there."

"Let's go," John said. He stood up and with his father following him, slowly moved into the direction of the sound. The horses stirred a little, but quieted down directly.

It was not difficult to go through the forest. The moon was still shining and the sky had already begun to lighten. Both made as little noise as possible by avoiding stepping on thin, dead twigs, and walking bent over to avoid being seen too easily.

After having gone a short distance they halted, surprised to see a small clearing with some primitive shelters from which the crying came. Looking at each other in sudden understanding, John was the first one to regain his composure.

"Come, Dad, let's talk with them. Maybe they need help," he said, and began to move to the largest shelter. At that moment, the shelter opened and a young woman, dressed in rags appeared. When she saw John and his father approaching, she shrieked, "Help! Louis, Henry, Guy, help! Strangers in our camp!"

John and his father kept moving, but had not gone more than three steps when all three shelters opened and several men appeared, some with knives in their hands. One of them, a man of middle age with a wild black beard, seemed to be their leader.

"There are only two," he said soothingly to the woman. "Louis, Guy, to their backs, and don't let them escape."

Two of the men rushed around John and his father, and took up a position at their backs. At a wink from the leader, two other men approached them from either side while the leader and the last man approached them from the front, halting a few yards away.

"Strangers, why are you disturbing our peaceful settlement?" the leader asked.

John's father did not wait for John to answer, and replied calmly, "No strangers, but brothers in Christ, I think."

Obviously, the men had not expected this answer because they looked at each other as if they were thoroughly amazed. Only their leader did not lose his composure. He looked them over and said contemptuously, "In times of persecution, true Christians don't walk around as well dressed as you. Who are you and where do you come from?"

"I'm a Huguenot who fled to Holland, but returned to liberate my father who was suffering for his faith on the galleys. The

Lord made me succeed, and now we are on our way to leave France, hopefully never to return again." John said, convinced that they were Huguenots in hiding, and desiring to win their confidence.

"If that is true, I'm sorry that I thought you to be our enemies," the leader apologized. "Come closer, sit down and let's get better acquainted."

"We'd like that, but I've first got to get our horses," John answered. "Dad, why don't you sit down and tell them why we are here?" Without waiting, he turned and walked back to the horses. The men at his back just stepped aside and let him go by.

When John returned with Prince and the mule, he found all the people gathered together around a small fire. There were six men, four women, five children of about twelve to fifteen years old, and two babies.

The story these people told was quite grim. A year ago they had lived peacefully together with a lot of Romanists in a small village in Languedoc. One morning, when they awoke, they found that soldiers were watching all the roads. A small group of soldiers, directed by some Romanist villagers, were searching the houses for Huguenots. They were brought to the church and guarded by soldiers while their houses were ransacked and their possessions were set on fire.

"We don't know what has happened to our brothers and sisters," said the leader of the group, who was called Guy,[72] "It is some comfort to us that only a few Romanist villagers helped the soldiers. Most of them were bystanders, terrified when they saw how our brothers and sisters were abused.

"We, who are sitting here, are thankful to the Lord that He let us escape in the most unusual ways. My wife and I dug ourselves into the manure pile. Nobody cared to search there. Others found different ways of escape, but it will be too long to tell all these stories. Anyhow, at night a few of us found each other and discovered a hiding place in an underground

---

[72] Guy is an abbreviation of Guillaume (William).

cave. The next nights we, the men, returned and were able to get a few more of our friends, whom we brought to our hiding place.

"We couldn't stay there so we decided to try to leave France. It took us eight months to come to this forest because we felt that traveling at night would be the safest. We have been here now over two months and we don't know what to do. Two of us went closer to the border, but discovered that the border area is well guarded by soldiers who patrol the roads and even sometimes the fields. The problem is that we have no food and winter is approaching.

"Last winter we had a very hard time with the cold and the snow and the lack of fuel. We don't think that we can survive another winter like that. We have prayed and thought but haven't yet figured out how to cross the border without being caught. Maybe you have an idea since you are fleeing France also, as you said!"

John and his father mentioned again that they also desired to cross the border. They told the group some of their adventures, and suggested that they would stay with them a few days to become better acquainted. All agreed and during the rest of the day they watched the daily life of the group.

Nearly all their time was used for getting food. The teenagers and two women disappeared into the forest to gather nuts and berries. Two men fetched water from a far away creek. A man and his wife inspected the snares they had set the previous day and returned with several rabbits and hares. Guy told them that once in a while they had succeeded in killing a deer.

The next morning, after lying awake most of the time in their efforts to think of a solution for these Huguenots, John's father suggested that they should talk again with Guy about the difficulty of crossing the border.

They found Guy at the edge of the clearing. He was skinning and cleaning half a dozen dead rabbits. When he saw them coming, he greeted them cordially. After a few sentences about the fine weather, John and his father waited patiently until he had finished his job. It did not take long. He cleaned his knife with a rag, put it in a sheath at his belt, and asked how they liked it in the camp.

"Well, I have some questions," John's father said, "or rather, I need some materials. If you can get them for us, I think I know how to get all of us safely across the border."

Guy's face showed that he did not believe it.

"Nobody will be as glad as I if you can do it. Tell me your plans and we'll do our utmost to get what you need."

"No, I don't think it wise to tell my plans now," John's father answered. "I don't want to raise false hopes, nor run the chance that my plans will leak out to the others before I'm ready. Listen. To execute my plans, I need enough rope to tie eight or ten prisoners. In addition, I want six to eight soldiers, complete with weapons and uniforms. It would be excellent if one of the soldiers was an officer."

First Guy smiled, thinking that it was meant to be a joke, but when he saw that John's father was serious, he shrugged his shoulders.

"What else do you want?" he asked sarcastically. "A couple of guns, and an army of Huguenots? Don't be a fool! You can't do anything with soldiers. They aren't any use to us. The Royal army will never buy their lives with a permit for us to cross the border."

"I'm not going to exchange them for a permit," John's father replied, "but I can't do anything without them. Now that I think about it, we won't have time to gather food when we start out for the border. Therefore, extra food is also needed. I'm sorry, Guy, that I have to ask your help without explaining my plan. Keep in mind that you don't have to listen to me. If you don't want to cooperate, just tell me, and we'll leave you alone. If you are willing to give us a try, I promise with my whole heart that John and I will stay with you to the end, until we are across the border or, if we fail, until the Lord takes us."

For a long time Guy considered the words of John's father. At last he said, "You know that I have to trust you. We are at the end of our tether. If we can't cross the border soon, we won't survive. I accept your proposal, provided you stick with us to the very end. I want you to take my place and I will be your right-hand man. Tonight we'll discuss the matter with the others. In the meantime, let's sit down and talk some more. We haven't heard anything about the fate of our brothers and sisters in France during the past year. Your story last night seems to indicate that important events have taken place, which may change our suffering."[73]

In the meeting that night, all agreed to cooperate with John's father. At his recommendation they made several important decisions. They decided to keep the horse, but to sell the mule for enough rope and more food. They also planned for six men to secretly patrol the area. When they saw single soldiers, they would take them prisoner and bring them, blindfolded, to their hiding place. Two men would stay behind and build a shelter for the prisoners. Every night they would have a prayer meeting for the success of their plans. As soon as they had everything they needed, a special meeting would be held where John's father would explain his plans.

---

[73] His deduction was wrong. The sufferings of the Huguenots ended only after the French Revolution in 1789 when, at last, they received freedom of religion.

20

PREPARATIONS FOR A DANGEROUS PLAN

THE whole camp was excited in anticipation of the meeting at night. It seemed to everyone that life had become much easier after John and his father joined the group. They had captured eight soldiers and kept them safely tied up in a kind of cage made from heavy branches. Feeding these captives was far less of a burden than they had expected after Louis managed to kill a deer. He hit its head with a sharp rock, which he happened to have in his hand when it sprang across the trail. The mule was sold to a farmer, not for money but for ropes and a large pile of food. They took the precaution to look for a farmer far away, two days walk from their hiding place.

Tonight, Guy had promised that they could eat enough to fill their stomachs because some of the food would spoil if kept longer. Every adult knew that John's father had a plan to cross the border, but all of them were wondering how they were going to use the prisoners in this plan. Many had tried to figure it out, but nobody had guessed it. All were in a cheerful mood, even the babies seemed to feel happy.

At the end of the day, a fire was made and some meat was broiled. Everybody, including the prisoners, received a piece of meat and a chunk of bread, which was more than they had eaten on one day for a long time. After their regular prayer meeting, which followed the meal, the whole group crowded together, watching John's father, who stood up and began to talk.

"Friends, the last four weeks we have done well, for which we give thanks to our Lord. We have captured eight soldiers with their gear, and we have enough food to last us for nearly a week. When John and I came here four weeks ago, Guy told us of your difficulty in crossing the border. I know that you are all anxious to hear how we are going to do it and why we need these eight soldiers. Well, I think that you can figure it out yourselves with a little bit of help. Consider what happens when a traveler wants to cross the border. Somewhere on the road he will be stopped by one or more soldiers. They will ask for his papers and he has to convince them that he belongs to the Roman church. Is there anybody who is not interrogated? Yes, of course, the soldiers! As soon as I had figured that out during the second night we were here, I understood that the crossing could be done very easily. We have just to disguise ourselves as soldiers.

"We, men, can easily do that, but it's impossible to disguise women and children as soldiers. It can't be done. They shouldn't therefore disguise themselves, but remain as they are, Huguenot women and children. Imagine! We, men, disguised as soldiers will bring a group of Huguenot women and children to prison. After having figured that out, I realized that we have another problem. All the men are soldiers and the women and children, Huguenot prisoners, but where are the Huguenot men? All groups of Huguenots guided along the roads contain men, and we don't have enough of them. We have our captured soldiers, though. I think that it is good for them to become Huguenot prisoners. We are going to use their uniforms and weapons to disguise ourselves, and we can't leave them behind. Therefore, we'll take them with us across the border disguised in our rags and release them as soon we have crossed the border to return to France." Everybody began to laugh about the soldiers in the role of Huguenots, but one of the men asked if that wasn't too dangerous.

"They may try to betray us when we come in contact with real soldiers," he said.

"I don't think so," John's father replied. "I think I can make them so scared that they'll keep their mouths shut, even when their own kind comes along." After some more discussion, it was decided that they would practice their roles the following three days and would leave on the fourth day.

*   *   *

The next days they spent diligently practicing the behavior of soldiers guiding along Huguenot prisoners. Fortunately, John's father had lots of experience, which he used in teaching them. Their greatest problem was that the men acted far too friendly for soldiers, and that the women had a difficult time showing their distress. At the end of the first day, they had mastered their behavior under regular circumstances rather well. The men had learned to yell at the women, and the women did not laugh but cried when the men shouted. Even the children knew how to act as Huguenot prisoners.

John's father insisted that John should act as the leading officer. He felt that it would be too dangerous for him, being an older man and not used to dealing with people of a higher status. The difficulty was that they had not been able to capture an officer so that John could only use the uniform of a regular foot soldier. He did not like it. It was most unlikely that an officer would do such a thing. At last, after a lot of thinking, he decided to wear his regular civilian suit and to justify it by emphasizing that he was a special envoy of King Louis.

After that was settled, they continued practicing the attitudes they were to use if they met patrollers and what they should do in emergencies. At the end of three days they felt confident that they could handle most situations without betraying themselves.

Early in the morning of the fourth day, John's father called together all the Huguenot men and explained that the time had come to dress up in the uniforms of the soldiers. At the same time, they would explain to their prisoners how they had to behave to escape with their life. The women and children were told to stay in the shelters during these scare tactics. Before they started, John's father took eight pieces of rope and made a running knot in everyone of them. He warned them to look as grim as possible to show the soldiers that they were desperate men, willing to do anything for their freedom.

The rest of their procedure was quite simple and worked far better than even the greatest optimist of them had expected. Two of them went to the cage where the prisoners were held. One of them was taken out and brought behind some bushes where he had to strip. One of the Huguenots dressed up in his uniform, and let the prisoner take his rags. Next they brought him to John's father who was surrounded by the other men, all looking grim.

After he had been interrogated about the patrols on the road to the border, their leading officers, their weapons and anything that could help the Huguenots, John's father gave them a choice.

"You better listen well," he said, speaking slowly, "for your life may be at stake if you make a mistake. Today we are going toward the border which we hope to cross tomorrow. We are dressed up in your uniforms as soldiers who are bringing Huguenots across the border. You and your friends are the Huguenots. You are not allowed to talk at all. If you exchange a single word with anybody but us, you will be knifed or hanged. In that case, we want to speed up the procedure and therefore we'll put this rope with a slip-knot around your neck so that your hanging won't delay us.

"Mind," he emphasized, "do not say a single word, not even when we meet a patrol on the road with your best friend. As soon as we are across the border at a safe place, we will let you go to return to France. We may even hand you some money. We give you the choice, you can cooperate with us or turn our offer down. If you turn it down, we will tie you up and leave you here, tied down to a tree. What do you choose?"

John's father did not have to say more. All the prisoners were so scared after this talk, surrounded by men with grim faces, that they hurried to tell them that they would cooperate in every way possible. When they had said so, they were tied to a tree, the next one was brought in, and the same scene repeated.

In the meantime, the women packed all the food in large parcels to be tied down on the backs of the prisoners. Now the worst part of their plan had to be done, the hands of the women and teenagers had to be tied. The two mothers with the babies were allowed to walk freely, except for a rope at their ankles that prevented them from running away. The other women and children were roped together with their wrists tied in front of them. Before this, John's father addressed all of them.

"Dear friends. The next two days will be a very difficult time for all of us, but for the women it will be far worse. We are walking freely, but they are tied up and can't defend themselves. May the Lord give us all the strength to bear our suffering cheerfully. As long as nobody is on the road we can talk and take it easy although we shouldn't make a lot of noise so that we can hear the patrollers as soon as possible. When we meet soldiers, remember that your life may be at stake if you look too cheerful. Guy, would you mind leading us in prayer before we leave?"

Twenty minutes later, they were walking along the post route. They had all agreed that John was best suited as their leader during these two days. He was riding Prince with his father walking next to him on his right side and Guy walking on his left side. Behind him the prisoners walked with glum faces, followed by the women. Two Huguenots walked at either side of the column, and the last one was at the rear of it.

21

JOHN CHALLENGED

THEY walked along the post route for several hours without meeting anyone. At noon, they went far enough inside the forest to be invisible to passers-by. The men hurriedly untied the women, and very soon everybody was sitting on the ground, talking and eating a few chunks of bread. It would have been too dangerous to untie the captured soldiers, but the Huguenots made sure that they were as comfortable as possible under the circumstances. They received a good share of the food and seemed to accept their role, knowing that as long as they cooperated they would be released within a few days. The women needed a rest and therefore they stayed for more than an hour at that spot.

A short time after lunch they met the first patrollers, four soldiers coming down the road. When the Huguenots saw them, their behavior changed drastically. The men yelled to the women, the women and the children sobbed and cried and John's face expressed contempt for such common soldiers.

The patrollers walked nonchalantly with their hands in their pockets. When they were close to John, he didn't wait for their questions, but growled to them, "Stand still! Didn't your officers teach you to greet respectfully when you meet your superiors?"

The soldiers, amazed to be addressed by a civilian, were nevertheless so used to being bullied by their superiors that they halted instinctively and greeted him respectfully. Their attitude became submissive when they realized that John was supported by five soldiers, leading a group of convicts. When John asked abruptly what company they were from, who their commanding officer was, and how far they were going down the road, he received polite answers. It seemed that this part of the road was patrolled only twice a day. The patrols consisted mostly of three or four foot soldiers, sometimes accompanied by a low-ranking officer. All this information agreed well with what the captive soldiers had told them.

John explained with a few words that he was an envoy of his majesty the king, with a special assignment. He ordered them to inspect the road over a length of six more hours walking.

The soldiers obeyed him directly after having given the proper salute. When they were far enough away they agreed between themselves that they were lucky not to have to report to such an officer every day.

The Huguenot group, glad that everything had gone so smoothly, stopped acting and continued their walk in the direction of the border, hopeful that further encounters would be as successful. John was not so sure. What would have happened if the soldiers had not obeyed him? After considering this possibility, he felt that it would be safer to have all the Huguenot soldiers close by when they encountered another patrol. When he brought this up during the next rest period, all agreed. They decided that when he halted the group, all the Huguenot soldiers would move forward without drawing attention.

Late in the afternoon when they intended to look for a shelter where they could stay during the night, they unexpectedly saw three soldiers leading two heavily shackled convicts around a curve in the road. John decided to try to do the same as in the previous encounter. He held his horse when they were close to the soldiers with the convicts and asked them curtly where they were going with the convicts, and what these men were accused of doing.

One of the soldiers, probably a low-ranking officer, replied with an insolent grin, "It isn't your business, Sir. You aren't our commanding officer. You aren't even an officer, I think!" He did not stop but kept walking along the side of the road to pass the group. Before John could give an order, they passed Guy who stuck his leg out, and tackled the soldier. John's father grabbed one of the other ones, but the third one ran away when he saw what happened to his friends.

He would have escaped, but Louis, who was an excellent runner, set off after the soldier and gained on him slowly. After they had turned a curve in the road, the soldier suddenly halted in an effort to fight him off. It did not help. Louis cannoned into him, and both fell on the ground where Louis soon had him under control. Panting he returned with his prisoner to the group where the wrists of the soldiers were tied together by Guy.

In the meantime, John questioned the convicts, a father and his son, both accused of being Huguenots. The soldiers were transferring them to a jail further away from the border. When John heard this, he dismounted Prince and told them that they were free.

"I can't explain everything at this moment, brothers," he said, "but you have to go with us and we'll tell you later." He urged the others to leave the road and to hide in the forest until a good shelter had been found.

"It's too dangerous to stay here. Anybody passing by would understand that something is amiss. Let's hide close to the road while my father and Guy, who have the most experience in the forest, look for a decent shelter for tonight. We'll go there as soon as they return, but now we must be quiet and not draw the attention of any unexpected passer-by."

A short time later, all were settled in an open clearing in the forest. The two Huguenots, still shackled, were watching everything with unbelieving eyes. While the women were untied, John and his father searched the pockets of the three soldiers. They found what they looked for, the key for the shackles. It was a small matter to take them off and to explain all the things that had happened. The father and his son could hardly believe that they were free again. They had tried to flee to Germany, but were caught close to the border. After listening to the plans of the Huguenots, they explained excitedly that they were anxious to join them in their effort to cross the border. All the Huguenots hastened to declare that they were very welcome in their small group.

The next morning, the Huguenots gave the newly captured soldiers the same choice as the other soldiers had had previously. Two of them consented, but the third one, who had been so impertinent to John, refused.

"You are Huguenots," he said insolently. "Your religion forbids you to kill me. Even if that wasn't so, you wouldn't have the guts to do it, anyhow. I haven't done anything wrong but obeyed my officer!"

"All right," John said, after considering the soldier's reply. "It's quite simple. We don't need your uniform. In fact, I wouldn't know what to do with you, anyway. We can't take you as a prisoner in your uniform and we don't have any civilian rags to dress you in. We'll tie you up and leave you here. If you are found, fine with me. It will be too late anyway to betray us, and if not, we gave you enough time to repent. Remember, even the murderer on the cross was forgiven."

Before they left the next day, the Huguenots tied the wrists and the feet of the soldier together and attached the end of the rope to a tree. They took the precaution to put a cloth over his head so that he could not draw attention by yelling, and left.

At their first rest period that day, John called Louis.

"I'm sorry but I'd appreciate you returning to the soldier we left behind. I think that he may have changed his mind and may be willing to cooperate now. Please, bring him here. We'll wait for you in this spot. You don't have to hurry because I think that we are less than four hours from the border."

"Fine, do you mind if I take Joseph with me? It makes the walking less boring and it may be helpful in keeping an eye on the soldier." After John had given his permission, they both took off to the previous night's shelter.

Several hours later Louis and Joseph returned with the prisoner. When they saw him, everybody had to laugh. The soldier obviously could not have walked up the road wearing his uniform. To make him look like a citizen, Louis had turned the jacket and pants inside out, and had cut off the sleeves of the jacket and part of the pants. It looked ridiculous, but nobody would suspect him of being a soldier anymore. Louis also reported that the soldier had changed his mind completely. He was willing to cooperate, and Louis had told him privately that he had better not break his promise if he wanted to stay alive.

Louis and Joseph needed only a short rest and they began the last part of their journey to the border shortly after noon. John and Guy warned them that it would be the most difficult part of their flight, and emphasized that the men especially must listen closely to their orders.

It was a surprise to all of them that they did not meet any patrollers during most of the afternoon, and they began to hope that they would be able to cross the border without any difficulties. It did not turn out that way.

They could not have been farther away from the border than an hour's walk when it happened. All at once, at least two dozen soldiers came around a curve in the road, preceded by a high-ranking officer on horseback. The appearance of this group came as a shock to all of them, but especially to John. All the captured soldiers had told him that the patrols consisted of small groups of soldiers only, but now he saw this large group! It flashed through his mind that if he couldn't bluff his way through, everything would be lost because the handful of Huguenots could never stand up against all these foot soldiers. He whispered to his father and Guy, "Please, stay close to me," and with a silent prayer in his heart, he rode boldly toward the foreign officer.

"I am Seigneur Dubois de Lisieux,[74] special envoy of His Majesty, the Grand Monarch, King Louis XIV. Please, introduce yourself." He was amazed to see that the officer was fairly young, no more than a few years older than himself, he estimated.

He probably belongs to the nobility, John thought contemptuously. He knew that young nobles frequently got high ranks due to the political influence of their family.

---

[74] John Dubois de Lisieux (French) = John van het Woudt van Lisieux (Dutch) = John of the Forest of Lisieux (English). John was born in a forest in the countryside of Lisieux.

"I am Chevalier de Montagneux, commissioned officer in the service of our King Louis XIV. My troops are assigned to patrol this post route," the officer replied politely.

"How is it possible that my men were able to catch these Huguenots while your men were patrolling the road?" John asked dourly. He saw the officer blush, but did not know if he was embarrassed or angry. He soon found out. All at once, the officer began to curse and to swear that he didn't take orders from royal spies, no matter how mighty they were.

"Guy, hit him across his mouth, and stop his foul talk," John cooly ordered the Huguenot, who obeyed him directly. "A good son of the Roman church isn't allowed to curse, and a good officer isn't allowed to despise the orders of my master, the king, whom I represent."

The officer, furious about the insult, tried to draw his sword, but John's father grasped both his arms and held them in his powerful hands. His soldiers began to grumble when they saw their officer treated as a prisoner. They unsheathed their swords and poniards, waiting for the command of their direct officers to attack. These men were, apparently, not sure what to do in this unusual situation. They felt that no common civilian would dare to attack an officer in the presence of his troop, and if this civilian had such a high rank, it was dangerous to resist him. After all, the penalty for insubordination was death.

John did not wait for the soldiers to attack him. He forced his horse past the officer toward the soldiers and stood up in the stirrups.

"Keep silent, all of you," he ordered curtly, "Put away your weapons and wait while I deal with your master!" He waited until quiet was restored, and then turned his horse a quarter circle so that he was facing the commanding officer and announced, speaking slowly in a loud, solemn voice, "Chevalier de Montagneux, I, Seigneur Dubois de Lisieux, special envoy of His Majesty King Louis XIV, accuse you of lese-majesty[75] by

---

[75] Lese-majesty = an offense against the king as head of the State.

Royal troops marching through the mountains
(Taken from an etching by Gérard)

neglecting your duty, by accusing His Majesty of spying on you, and by disobeying me, His Majesty's envoy."

Everybody present, including the officer's troops, listened breathlessly, not daring to interfere. The officer tried to speak, but when he opened his mouth, Guy held his hand over it so that only some unintelligible sounds were heard. At that moment Joseph saw that one of the soldiers, forced to act as a Huguenot, intended to yell something to the officer's men. Just in time Joseph grasped the rope tied around the soldier's neck, and pulled so hard that the gliding knot cut off the prisoner's breath.

"Don't say anything," he growled to the soldier, "or I'll throttle you." He released the rope slightly so that the soldier could breathe freely. Convinced that the man had learned his lesson, Joseph looked around, but saw that all the other prisoners were keeping quiet.

John turned to his father, Guy, and Louis, and ordered them curtly to tie the officer to the horse, and to gag him so that he couldn't yell curses and obscenities anymore. While these men were engaged in executing his orders, he turned to the officer's soldiers.

"Who is the second in command?" he asked. A large fellow came forward.

"I am, Sir," he said, evidently at a loss of what to do.

"You see that I've arrested your master. I did it at the command of his royal highness, the king," John said, and added haughtily, "I'm not used to showing my authority to common foot soldiers, but I'll do it this time so that you'll understand that disobedience to my commands will be punished severely. Remember, the arms of His Majesty King Louis XIV are long."

"Yes, Sir," the soldier replied meekly.

"Can you read?" John asked.

"No, Sir. I can't, Sir," the man retorted, surprised at the question.

"Can any of you read?" John asked in a loud voice, addressing the officer's soldiers. All of them remained standing without answering, except for one soldier, who hesitantly mentioned that he could read just a little.

"Come here," John commanded curtly. The man came forward until he stood close to John's horse, Prince. John took his recommendation from his breast pocket, opened it, held it on his knee and told the soldier to read it aloud. It became clear to John, that the soldier could hardly read at all, as he had expected. He knew how to take advantage of it. Impatiently he took the letter away.

"What do you think? I haven't the whole day to let you spell out every word of this letter. I will show you that it is a letter from his majesty the king." He pointed with his finger to the words King Louis XIV and told the soldier to spell it aloud. After that, he let him spell the word Huguenots and then returned the letter to his breast pocket again.

"You have all heard that my commission is from His Majesty King Louis XIV, and that he has given me the assignment to catch Huguenots. Everybody who disobeys me, disobeys his majesty, the king.

"Tell me," he commanded the second in command, "where are you going at this time of the day?"

"I'm not completely sure, Sir, but I understand that we were being transferred to Grenoble."

"It is no use to delay your transfer," John declared. "I command you to continue to Grenoble. You will take Chevalier de Montagneux with you. You can remove his gag tonight, provided he doesn't talk. If he speaks, you'll have to gag him again. In Grenoble, you must surrender him to the governor of the city. Tell him that I, Seigneur Dubois, command him to keep this man in jail until I arrive. Now, depart!"

The soldier looked somewhat puzzled, but seeing that John was in earnest, he went to the horse on which his officer was bound, took the reins, gave an order to his group, and began to walk past the Huguenot group.

After the last one of them was out of sight, John turned to his group and smiled.

"I'm glad it went so smoothly," he said simply. "I guess that we have another hour's walk to reach the border. Let's go, for I am afraid as long as we are in France."

Without further adventures they walked another hour and then untied the women. They still didn't feel safe and continued walking more than two hours longer. There they found a safe hiding place where they nearly collapsed from exhaustion. After making the soldiers as comfortable as possible, all went to sleep, too tired to think or to do anything.

22

THE DUKE OF SAVOY

IT was late in the morning when John woke up. The sun was shining in his face and he heard people softly moving around. He did not like to wake up, but he forced himself to open his eyes, knowing that a lot had to be arranged. His father was sitting next to him, contentedly looking at a small campfire which was burning a hundred feet away. When he heard John moving, he turned quickly to him and smiled.

"Well, son, it took a long time for you to wake up," he said teasingly. "The women have already given me breakfast. You better get moving if you don't want to miss out on it." Slowly, John sat up. First he looked without much interest at the women busy at the campfire, then his eyes took in their surroundings. He was surprised that they were on the slope of a low mountain. Seeing it, he understood why the last part of their journey had been so tiring. They had been walking on a gradually climbing road!

"I'm happy that we made it across the border," he said to his father, "but I feel so tired that I hate to get up."

"Don't," his father replied smiling while he stood up. "I'll get something for you to eat and that'll help a lot. For the time being we are safe, I think. We have to take care of our prisoners and make plans where to go next, but we can take it easy, though."

A short time later he returned with food and some water. While John was eating and drinking, Guy came down the slope from behind some bushes.

"Good morning, John," he said cheerfully. "I've told Louis to watch the road and to report anything that seems dangerous. We are all ready to move again. What do you want us to do?"

"First, we have to hold a meeting," John suggested, embarrassed that older men like Guy and his own father expected him to give advice.

"All right, John," Guy replied. "I'll tell everybody to come here. That is easier for you."

They must have been waiting for John to wake up because he was all at once surrounded by his happy, cheerful friends, all laughing and talking together. He had never seen them as excited as they were now and it took his father and Guy quite some time before they had persuaded them to sit down quietly on the grass. At last, Guy was the only one standing. He looked at all the faces turned to him and began to talk.

"Friends, the Lord has been merciful to us. He brought us safely across the border and we must praise and thank Him." He led them in prayer and spontaneously they began to sing Psalms. Guy recited from his heart a few Bible verses of thanksgiving and afterward they sang another Psalm. They continued the singing and reciting of the Bible for nearly two hours and then Guy began to speak again, thanking John that he had led them so well. He especially praised John for dealing so effectively with the high-ranking officer and his large group of soldiers. John turned crimson.

"Stop it, Guy," he protested. "You don't know how scared I was. I knew that we would all be made prisoners if we couldn't bluff our way through. I don't know why, but I certainly felt that it was the only way of dealing with that officer. The Lord must have guided us all because none of us did anything that could have betrayed us."

His protest didn't help. Several adults jumped up and began to tell how thankful they were that John had joined them. It was difficult to understand their words, all talking at the same time but everyone, including John, understood their gratitude. Guy only smiled while this was going on and waited until silence was restored. Then he explained briefly that they had to make a decision on how to proceed. They were now in the duchy of Savoy, but could not stay there. The Duke, Victor Amadeus II, would not persecute them, but he would consider them unwelcome guests because he could not afford to antagonize King Louis XIV by sheltering French Huguenots.

After a short discussion, the group made their decision. No one wanted to stay in Savoy, but they knew that they would be welcome in Geneva, the famous city where John Calvin had taught for so many years. When someone asked how far it was to Geneva, Guy assured them that it would not be too difficult to go there.

After that decision was made, all looked at John, and Guy expressed their mutual desire in a few words.

"John, all of us would love it if you and your father would come with us. We trust and love you and feel that, the Lord willing, we'll arrive safely in Geneva if you are our guide." Everybody looked expectantly at John, hoping that he would say yes. John just shook his head, touched by their friendliness, but he had made up his mind that since he was so close to the court of the duke, he must deliver the letter of Mr. Heinsius. When they kept waiting, apparently expecting a kind of speech, he turned to them.

"Friends, I'm deeply touched by your confidence in me. I would like to go with you because it will be difficult to say goodbye after all the dangers we went through together. Nevertheless, it's impossible. I've got to go to Turin, the capital of Savoy. Maybe my father is willing to remain with you, but I can't." His father, hearing for the first time that John did not intend to stay with the group, did not hesitate and said briefly that he would stay with his son, come what may. It was a great disappointment, but everybody accepted John's decision without grumbling.

Next, they discussed what to do with the soldiers. The group was afraid that they might turn against them if they were all released simultaneously. After having listened to different opinions, Guy at last suggested to let only two or three go at a time. Everybody agreed, knowing no better solution. They brought the soldiers to the meeting where Guy informed them that every day two or three of them would be released, after they had sworn an oath not to bother Huguenots anymore.

It was too late in the afternoon when the meeting was over to start their trip to Geneva. They decided to stay one more night at that spot and to leave the next morning.

*   *   *

A week later John and his father arrived in Turin. They found a modestly priced inn where they rented a room. It was difficult to make themselves understood because neither John nor his father understood Italian, and the innkeeper did not speak French. However, as soon as John showed a few French coins, the innkeeper smiled and took them to a small room, indicating by gestures that they could sleep there. When they went a little later to the large room downstairs, the innkeeper, again with gestures, told them to sit at a small table, and before he left, a maidservant brought two steaming plates of soup.

While they were eating, they were joined by a friendly man dressed in simple clothes. He sat down and told them in French that his name was Philippe Dutoit. He lived a few houses down the street. The innkeeper had contacted him to act as a translator.

"What can I do for you, gentlemen?" he asked after he had introduced himself.

John and his father were agreeably surprised that the innkeeper had taken such good care of them. Without giving any details, they told him their names, and simply mentioned that they had arrived from France.

"I thought so," Philippe replied. "King Louis XIV regularly sends messengers since our Duke became his ally. The trouble is that few people in Turin can speak French since the king forced our duke to forbid any French Huguenot refugees from staying in Savoy. More than three thousand French Waldenses and seven of their ministers had to leave and went to Germany."[76]

Philippe appeared to be quite proud of the city he lived in. He explained that the Italian name was Torino, and that the bridge across the river Po was one of the most famous bridges

---

[76] This happened in 1698. As a result, the Protestant population of Savoy was so much reduced that in the time of this story it contained fewer than twelve hundred men who were able to carry weapons.

in the neighborhood. He also mentioned the beauty of the duke's palace. Here John interrupted him, and asked him to be his translator when he visited the duke.

"Oh, no," said Philippe. "I don't like to enter the duke's palace. You don't need a translator, anyway, because the duke himself and many of his officials can speak French fluently." John tried to find out why Philippe was afraid to go to the palace, but Philippe avoided his questions by talking more about Turin.

His conversation at least served a good purpose. John heard the names of several court officials who were in close contact with the duke. At last, after this amiable conversation, Philippe left, but told them where they could find him, if needed.

The next morning, John went to the palace, hoping to be able to deliver his letter personally into the hands of the duke. He was quite nervous because he wasn't sure how to handle the situation.

Mr. De Groot had told him that the duke was allied with King Louis XIV mainly because he needed the king's protection. However, he had mentioned to him confidentially that the letter was written in an effort to persuade the duke to join the alliance against the French king. The war between Holland and France complicated everything, he felt.

It would be foolish to tell anybody that he came with a message of the United Republic, the arch enemy of France. He was sure that he would never get access to the duke if his servants suspected that he came from Holland. However, after his talk with Philippe, he had realized that a messenger from King Louis was quite common. That knowledge was a welcome piece of information and would make it possible to see the duke privately, he hoped.

When he came to the large, open doors of the duke's palace he tried to walk in, but was halted by two soldiers, standing watch at each side of the door. They said something to him in Italian, which he didn't understood. He retorted in French by naming the Count of Saluzzo, the duke's general. One of the soldiers went away, and returned a short time later with a civilian who addressed John politely in French.

Victor Amadeus II of Savoy (1665-1732)

He asked his name and the purpose of his visit. John gave his name, John Dubois de Lisieux, mentioned that he had arrived the previous day from France, and had used the name of the Count de Saluzzo only because he knew that the count could speak French. The real purpose of his visit, however, was to see His Highness Duke Victor Amadeus II.

"I have an urgent message for his highness, the duke," he added haughtily, confident that it was the proper attitude for a messenger of King Louis.

The man turned around and said only, "Please, follow me, Sir." After having gone through several corridors and rooms, he halted in front of a door, knocked, and after someone inside had given permission to enter, opened the door and announced, "Sir, John Dubois de Lisieux, a messenger from France, who desires to see his highness Duke Victor Amadeus." He stepped aside and held the door open for John. After John had entered, he closed the door behind him.

In the room a man was sitting behind a writing table. He stood up and introduced himself.

"I'm the secretary of His Highness Duke Victor Amadeus II of Savoy," he said in French. "I understand that you are a messenger of King Louis of France, and that you want to give your message to his highness. Please, sit down and let's discuss your message." He gestured to a chair in front of the desk and seated himself behind it again.

"I'm afraid that you aren't acquainted with the rules of this court. His highness, the duke, desires to be disturbed as little as possible by messengers. Therefore, he made the rule that all messengers — in fact, all visitors — must present their messages to me. I sort them out and present them to his highness, the duke."

"I'm sorry, Sir," John replied. "My message is strictly confidential. I'm not allowed to give it to anybody but the duke without anyone else being present." The secretary tried for a long time to persuade John to give him the message, but John stubbornly refused.

At last, the secretary gave up and left through a door at the other side of the room. John heard some voices, but he returned fairly soon, and asked John to go through the door where he would find the duke, ready to give him an audience.

The duke, a young man,[77] stood in the middle of the room, waiting impatiently for John to introduce himself.

"Your highness, my name is John Dubois," John said, reciting the speech he had prepared and memorized beforehand. "I requested this interview pretending that I am a messenger from France. I'm not, although I traveled through France to Savoy. I'm a messenger of Mr. Heinsius, the Pensionary of the United Republic, who wanted this letter to be delivered into your hands." John took the letter he had carried for such a long time, went down on one knee, and presented it to the duke.

"I apologize for the crumpled appearance of the letter," he added. "I had to carry it in the lining of my jacket for safety reasons."

---

[78] The Duke Victor Amadeus II (1675-1732) was thirty-seven years old at the time of this story.

Geneva in the seventeenth century

The duke looked surprised, but took the letter and looked at its seals. He thought for a moment while John was standing patiently before him. At last he looked directly at John, not unkindly, and said, "Mr. Dubois, you mentioned that you traveled through France. Why didn't you go the easier road through Germany and Switzerland?"

"I'm the secretary of a Dutch gentleman, Mr. De Groot. Mr. Heinsius sent him as a special envoy of the United Republic to Paris. When we were there, the United Republic and their allies sent the Declaration of War to King Louis XIV and Mr. De Groot had to return speedily to Holland. Before he left, he gave me this letter and asked me to take it to you."

"You've done well, Mr. Dubois," the duke replied, went to the door and opened it.

"Mr. Montoux, please join us," he called. "I want you to take some notes."

Within a moment, the gentleman who had questioned John prior to his interview with the duke entered.

"This is Mr. Montoux, my secretary, Mr. Dubois," the duke said. "We're very much interested to hear how King Louis XIV and his people reacted when they received the Declaration of

War. You can discuss it with Mr. Montoux. In the meantime, I'll read this letter.

"Mr. Montoux, I want to see you after your talk with Mr. Dubois. Please make sure that he has comfortable lodgings. I want to see him again tomorrow morning," the duke commanded before he left.

"Well, Mr. Dubois, let's go to my office where it is more comfortable," Mr. Montoux suggested.

As soon as they were seated, Mr. Montoux explained the difficult situation of the duke of Savoy. He didn't like being the ally of King Louis XIV but was forced into it because Savoy was such a small Duchy that France could run it underfoot within a few weeks.[78] Nevertheless, the duke, being a brave man, was considering joining the Dutch alliance, if he could do it without too much risk. For that reason, it was of the utmost importance for him to know how the people in France had reacted.

Hearing this, John decided that it might be encouraging for them to hear that the Huguenots had begun to defend themselves. The next few hours, John gave his impressions of life in Versailles, the empty harbor of Dunkerque, and the liberation of the prisoners of the Abbé du Chaila. Mr. Montoux became quite excited about all this news. The story of the Abbé especially made a deep impression on him.

Before John left his office, he also mentioned that he had run out of money. He asked Mr. Montoux if he could arrange for a small loan, to be repaid as soon as he had returned to Holland. Hearing this, Mr. Montoux could not help laughing.

"Your information is so valuable that I'm certain the duke will be willing to help you in every respect. Don't worry about it. I'll let one of our servants go with you to your lodging. He'll arrange with the innkeeper for you to stay for free, or rather that our duke will pay for you. Goodbye. I hope to see you tomorrow."

---

[78] Mr. Rebenac Feuquieres, the representative of King Louis XIV in Savoy, declared officially to Duke Victor Amadeus: ". . . that the King, his master, could find the means to exile all heretics from the Valleys with fourteen thousand men and keep the Valleys himself if the Duke of Savoy would remain to be unwilling to do it."

23

HOME AT LAST

IT was Sunday morning. The members of the French Reformed Church[79] in Amsterdam were quietly waiting for the start of the worship service. Mrs. Marguerite Chatelaine, the minister's wife, and her adopted daughter Manette, John's sister, were sitting in the first pew of the right wing of the church. Manette always liked that place. They were close enough to the pulpit to give the minister their full attention and at the same time could see most of the congregation.

While the organ was playing softly, the elders and the minister entered. The congregation rose to their feet and the elders remained standing in their pews in front of the church while the minister ascended the pulpit. The organ stopped playing, and after a silent prayer, the minister welcomed the congregation in the name of the Lord. After the singing of a Psalm, the congregation seated itself comfortably in anticipation of the Bible reading, which was a common part of their liturgy.

Everyone watched the minister, who had turned several pages to find the proper passage in the Bible and now looked up to announce the texts he was going to recite. Suddenly, the congregation heard the door in the rear of the church open and saw the minister's face change. First, he appeared annoyed about the interruption. Then, all at once his whole face brightened and with a smile, he addressed the congregation.

"Brothers and Sisters, two guests have entered our worship service." Afterward, he could not remember what more he had said, but everybody heard him joyously call out that John had

---

[79] The French Reformed Church = *De Walsche Gemeinte* (Old Dutch).

returned, before he rushed down the pulpit to hug him. However, before the minister could reach John, Manette had already jumped from her place. She raced along the path between the pews toward him and his companion. She did not even look at John, but threw her arms around the neck of the stranger, laughing and crying, "Oh, Daddy, you have come at last." The stranger hugged her with tears in his eyes and a glad smile while the minister and his wife were hugging John, and the congregation left their pews and watched the encounter with happy faces.

At last the man, whom everyone now understood to be the father of John and Manette, stopped hugging Manette. He did not let her small hands go, but held them in his own large hands.

"I didn't intend to interrupt your worship service," he said timidly in French. "I couldn't help it. I haven't seen my girl for so many years and I'm so happy that the Lord brought us together again, that I can't even feel real sorry for it."

"Be welcome in our worship service," the minister said with shining eyes, so that John's father felt that he really was welcome. "But now, let's continue the worship service. Afterward we can talk more." He hurried back to the pulpit, the congregation seated themselves again, and the minister led them in a service of thanksgiving.

*   *   *

It was the following day, quite late in the morning, when John went to the office of Mr. De Groot. He felt somewhat embarrassed that he had overslept, but everybody had assured him that it was understandable. The last two days had been incredibly tiring. He and his father had arrived in Utrecht late Saturday night after the last coach to Amsterdam had already left. The next coach would leave early on Monday morning, they found out. It was a big disappointment because they were both anxious to get home as soon as possible. Therefore, John's father had readily agreed to walk home when John mentioned that it would take no more than eight hours.

Luckily they had taken some food with them because it took several hours longer than John had estimated.

The trip and the joyful homecoming on Sunday after which they had been busy talking and meeting with the other Huguenots, were the cause of his late oversleeping. In fact, it was not too bad, he thought, because now Mr. De Groot would already be in his office.

He smiled when he recalled that neither his adopted father nor his friends had heard of the dangerous situation for Mr. De Groot in Paris. They knew only that he had returned safely from a business trip to France because Manette had mentioned that he had visited her and their adopted parents personally to explain why John had insisted staying in France longer. Mr. De Groot had explained that he didn't know when John would return, but had emphasized that they should not worry because it could take several months. It was dangerous in France for John, he had said.

Every week he had sent John's wages to Manette, and the last few weeks he had even come himself to encourage her.

When John opened the familiar office door, the clerks looked up, as they always did when visitors walked in. When they saw John standing at the door, they showed their surprise by excitedly jumping up. They shook his hands, pounded his shoulders, and shouted words of welcome, affection, and surprise in loud voices.

They like me and they were worried about me, John thought, amazed that he never had expected that. He tried to answer all their questions during the tumultuous noise, when suddenly everybody quieted down. Mr. De Groot had suddenly appeared behind John in the hallway. The clerks were astonished. They had never seen him smiling as broadly as he did now, seeing John. He grabbed John's shoulders and turned him around so that he could see his face.

"How happy I am that you have returned safely," he said affectionately.

"Mr. Cornelissen," he addressed the oldest of the clerks, "This is a day of celebration. Get a bottle of wine and drink it with your colleagues to the health of this young man who escaped for the second time from France. John, please, come to my office and tell me everything."

A few hours later, John ended the story of his adventures by giving Mr. De Groot a letter.

"This is a secret letter from Duke Victor Amadeus II of Savoy in which he explains how dangerous his situation is. I saw him two times. The last time he asked me to tell Mr. Heinsius that he is watching the situation closely, and will join the Alliance as soon as he can without being overrun by the troops of King Louis.[80] He was nice enough to pay for our return by regular mail coaches, and so we arrived in Amsterdam yesterday morning."

"I'll personally give this letter to Mr. Heinsius," Mr. De Groot responded. "I'll also tell him of the excellent service you have done for our country and that you have liberated your father. I'm thankful to the Lord that you have returned safely. May He bless our efforts in our struggle with Louis XIV for the survival of His church."

---

[80] The Duke of Savoy joined the Alliance six months later.

EPILOGUE

HISTORY OF THE CHURCH REFORMATION IN FRANCE

The history of the Church of Christ in France is relatively unknown in spite of its glorious past. The faithful perseverance and testimony of its members during horrible persecutions are a source of praise and encouragement for all Christians. The courage and steadfastness of the French children in particular during these gruesome years has been unequaled during all the known history of the Church of Christ. Even now they are bright examples for all Christian teenagers, who in an anti-Christian world are under serious peer pressure and exposed to the temptations of alcohol and drugs and to a deteriorated morality.

The following is a brief description of the early history of the Church of Christ in France.

The Protestants in France were named Huguenots. The true meaning of this name is not certain, but the word is probably derived from a word that means Covenanters. The gospel spread fast after the beginning of the Reformation in Germany in 1517. In cooperation with the French kings, the mighty Roman Catholic Church tried its utmost to stop the progress of the Reformation using blatant persecutions. The first French martyr, an Augustinian monk, named Jean Valliers, was burned alive at the stake in Paris in 1523. It was the start of severe persecution in which thousands and thousands of Christians, men and women, children and old men, laymen and clergy were tortured and burned alive. Many historical sources tell of their faithful adherence to the Lord Jesus Christ.

The suffering in France was borne with Psalm singing. The death of the martyrs was a singing death; they sang while being burned alive. The Psalms of these Christian witnesses, sung in smoke and fire, became known, and everybody began to sing them. Even in Paris one day three or four thousand people sang them in public despite the rage of the king. The persecutions did not stop the progress of the Gospel. Less than thirty years after the death of the first martyr, the Huguenot Church had nearly half a million members and a few years later at least 40 percent of the total French population were Huguenots.

The first synod met in Paris in 1559. Obviously, they had to meet in secret because during those times, the Kings Francis I (reigned 1515-1547) and Henry II (reigned 1547-1559) tried to liquidate the church. In spite of these difficulties, the synod was able to complete a heavy and important workload. It agreed upon a creed and established rules for governing the church, all based on Calvinistic, biblical principles.

During this period a large number of nobles joined the Huguenot Church. Their leader was the well-known Caspard de Coligny. They were opposed by the Romanist nobles and their leader, De Guise. King Charles IX (reigned 1560-1574), who was wholly under the influence of his mother, Catherine de Medici, sided with the Romanists. The struggle between these two parties came to an end with the bloody St. Bartholomew's night (Aug. 23-24, 1572). During that night and the next few days more than thirty thousand Huguenots were murdered, including De Coligny.

Until 1589 France was ravaged by civil war, murder, and persecution. During that year, the protestant leader King Henry IV made a compromise; he became a Roman Catholic convert, and was acknowledged as France's legal king by both parties. His main goal was then to maintain peace in his country, and so he gave special privileges to the Huguenots in the Edict of Nantes (1598). It allowed a kind of freedom of religion unknown in the western world, except in The Netherlands. The Huguenots were allowed to practice their religion in a certain number of cities, and they were recognized — to a certain extent — as an armed political party. In addition, they received some fortified towns, like the harbor town of La Rochelle.

However, these special privileges quickly became a threat to the very existence of the nation because the Huguenots were allowed to form their own state inside the nation. Cardinal Richelieu (1585-1642), then Prime Minister, understood this well. Gradually he canceled all privileges and conquered the fortified cities of the Huguenots.

Severe persecution of the Huguenots resumed during the reign of Louis XIV, the Sun King (reigned 1643-1715) because he wanted to be an absolute monarch. He expected to achieve his goal by allowing

186

only one church in France, the Roman Catholic Church. He followed the recommendations of his confessor, the notorious Pere La Chaise, and supported any action that would result in the Huguenots returning to the Roman Church including persecution, bribery, and murder.

The life of the Huguenots became unbearable after the revocation of the Edict of Nantes, and many of them tried to leave France. King Louis, who knew that the Huguenots were his most diligent and hard workers, did not want them to leave and used his soldiers to turn them back at the borders. Our story took place during those times.

In spite of the soldiers, approximately one-half million Huguenots succeeded in their flight. They were received and supported by the Christians in Switzerland, England, The Netherlands, and Brandenburg.

In the famous war of the Camisards (1702-1704), the Huguenots in a mountainous country of southern France called the Cevennes, tried to defend their lives. They are known as Camisards because they often wore a shirt (camisole) over their clothes during nightly attacks. Their courage and discipline were unrivaled. Although their army consisted of fewer than two thousand five hundred soldiers, a French army of twenty thousand men with famous generals and supported by fifty-two battalions of recruits could barely subdue them. After this war, the Reformed Church in France appeared to be nearly completely liquidated. However, after a few years a revival occurred and although the persecution continued, it was less bloody than before. The church began to grow again under the leadership of Antoine Court and the ministers he and others trained. The congregations had thousands of members again during the latter part of the eighteenth century. At last, in 1790, the Huguenots were given freedom of religion. Nevertheless, a spirit of rationalism had contaminated the church so much that it lost most of its members during and after the French revolution.

At present, the French Reformed Church is again active in its mission work, but continues to be very small.

Other Books from Inheritance Publications

Quintus by R. Weerstand
A Story About the Persecution of Christians
at the Time of Emperor Nero

The history of the Church in A.D. 64 is written with blood and tears. This book, based on historical facts, relates what happened in Rome in the summer of that year. It is a gripping chronicle. In the story we meet Quintus, the central character. He is a typical Roman boy, who through a number of ordeals experiences the grace of God.

Time: A.D. 64 **Age: 12-99**
Cat. Nr. IP 1270 **Can.\$8.95 U.S.\$7.90**

William of Orange - The Silent Prince
by W.G. Van de Hulst

F. Pronk in *The Messenger*: If you have ever wondered why Dutch Reformed people of former generations felt such strong spiritual ties with Dutch royalty, this is a "must" reading. In simple story form, understandable for children ages 10 and up, the Dutch author, wellknown for Christian children's literature, relates the true story of the origin of Dutch royalty. It all began with William of Nassau (1533-1584) . . . He dedicated his life and lost it for the cause of maintaining and promoting Protestantism in The Netherlands.

for age 9 - 99 **ISBN 0-921100-15-9 Can.\$8.95 U.S.\$7.90**

Salt in His Blood
The Life of Michael De Ruyter
by William R. Rang

The greatest Dutch Admiral is an example of Christian love and piety, and fascinating because of his many true adventures as a sailer-boy, captain, and pirate-hunter.

Time: 1607 - 1676 **Age: 10-99**
ISBN 0-921100-59-0 **Can.\$10.95 U.S.\$9.90**

Anak, the Eskimo Boy by Piet Prins

F. Pronk in *The Messenger*: Anak is an Eskimo Boy, who with his family, lives with the rest of their tribe in the far north. The author describes their day-to-day life as they hunt for seals, caribou and walruses. Anak is being prepared to take up his place as an adult and we learn how he is introduced to the tough way of life needed to survive in the harsh northern climate. We also learn how Anak and his father get into contact with the white man's civilization. . . This book makes fascinating reading, teaching about the ways of Eskimos, but also of the power of the Gospel. Anyone over eight years old will enjoy this book and learn from it.

for age 8 - 99 **ISBN 0-921100-11-6 Can.\$6.95 U.S.\$6.30**

The Spanish Brothers by Deborah Alcock
A Tale of the Sixteenth Century

"He could not die thus for his faith. On the contrary, it cost him but little to conceal it. What, then, had they which he had not? Something that enabled even poor, wild, passionate Gonsalvo to forgive and pray for the murderers of the woman he loved. What was it?"

The Spanish Brothers is an accurate historical account of the rise, progress, and downfall of the Protestant Church in Spain. Especially may be mentioned the story of the two great Autos-da-fé (Acts of Faith — parade and execution of "heretics") at Seville. Only what concerns the personal history of the brothers and their family is fiction.

But what is not fiction, but absolute truth, is that God repays His faithful servants a hundred-fold, even in this life, for anything they do or suffer for His Name's sake.

Time: 1550-1565 — Age: 14-99
ISBN 1-984666-02-x — Can.$14.95 U.S.$12.90

With Wolfe in Canada by G.A. Henty

Christine Farenhorst in *Christian Renewal*: Dubbed 'Prince of Story Tellers' and 'The Boy's Own Historian' by his peers, Henty (1832-1902), was certainly worthy of both epithets. A master at retelling history, he recreated the taking of Quebec by the English with personal and exciting strokes of the pen in this particular volume.

Although James Walsham, the young protagonist in this tale, is fictional, the dates and sequence of events are all accurate. James is a paragon of virtue — honest, forthright, courageous and diligent in all duty — in short, a wonderful model to emulate for any reader.

Inheritance Publications is to be heartily commended for republishing not only this particular novel, which has a distinct Canadian flavor (with a British aftertaste), but also for bringing other Henty volumes out of the woodwork.

Highly recommended.

Time: 1750-1765 — Age: 14-99
Cloth ISBN 0-921100-86-8 — Can.$28.95 U.S.$19.99
Paperback ISBN 0-921100-87-6 — Can.$20.95 U.S.$13.99

Journey Through the Night by Anne De Vries

After the second world war, Anne De Vries, one of the most popular novelists in The Netherlands, was commissioned to capture in literary form the spirit and agony of those five harrowing years of Nazi occupation. The result was Journey Through the Night, a four volume bestseller that has gone through more than thirty printings in The Netherlands.

"An Old Testament Professor of mine who bought the books could not put them down — nor could I."

— Dr. Edwin H. Palmer

Time: 1940-1945 — Age: 10-99
ISBN 1-984666-21-6 — Can.$19.95 U.S.$14.90

When The Morning Came by Piet Prins
Struggle for Freedom Series 1

D. Engelsma in the *Standard Bearer*: This is reading for Reformed children, young people, and (if I am any indication) their parents. It is the story of 12-year-old Martin Meulenberg and his family during the Roman Catholic persecution of the Reformed Christians in The Netherlands about the year 1600. A peddlar, secretly distributing Reformed books from village to village, drops a copy of Guido de Brès' *True Christian Confession* — a booklet forbidden by the Roman Catholic authorities. An evil neighbor sees the book and informs . . .

for age 9 - 99   **ISBN 0-921100-12-4   Can.$9.95 U.S.$8.90**

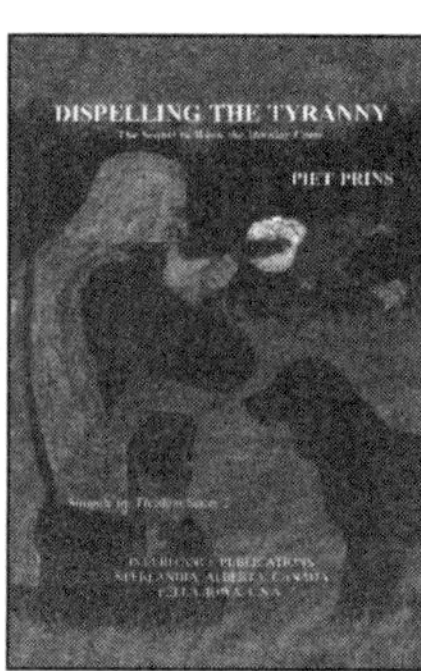

Dispelling the Tyranny by Piet Prins
Struggle for Freedom Series 2

"Father! Mother! I saw Count Lodewyk! He rode through the city on a black horse!" Martin shouted, as he dashed into the humble home where his parents were eating supper. "The cavalry followed him, and everywhere he went the people cheered him on!" Martin's eyes sparkled with excitement.   for age 9 - 99

ISBN 0-921100-40-X   Can.$9.95 U.S.$8.90

Augustine, The Farmer's Boy of Tagaste by P. De Zeeuw

C. MacDonald in *The Banner of Truth*: Augustine was one of the great teachers of the Christian Church, defending it against many heretics. This interesting publication should stimulate and motivate all readers to extend their knowledge of Augustine and his works.

J. Sawyer in *Trowel & Sword*: . . . It is informative, accurate historically and theologically, and very readable. My daughter loved it (and I enjoyed it myself). An excellent choice for home and church libraries.

Time: 354 - 430 A.D.   **Age: 9-99**

ISBN 0-921100-05-1   **Can.$7.95 U.S.$6.90**

The Escape by A. Van der Jagt

The Adventures of Three Huguenot Children
Fleeing Persecution

F. Pronk in *The Messenger*: This book . . . will hold its readers spellbound from beginning to end. The setting is late seventeenth century France. Early in the story the mother dies and the father is banished to be a galley slave for life on a war ship. Yet in spite of threats and punishment, sixteen-year-old John and his ten-year-old sister Manette, refuse to give up the faith they have been taught.

Time: 1685 - 1695 **Age: 12-99**
ISBN 0-921100-04-3 **Can.$11.95 U.S.$9.95**

The Secret Mission by A. Van der Jagt

A Huguenot's Dangerous Adventures
in the Land of Persecution

In the sequel to our best-seller, *The Escape,* John returns to France with a secret mission of the Dutch Government. At the same time he attempts to find his father.

Time: 1702-1712 **Age: 12-99**
ISBN 0-921100-18-3 **Can.$14.95 U.S.$10.95**

How They Kept The Faith
by Grace Raymond

A Tale of the Huguenots of Languedoc

Eglantine and Rene grew up together in a Huguenot family. Already at a young age they are committed to become each other's life's partner. When persecution breaks out they each must endure their individual struggles to remain faithful to God and to each other. A must for teenagers and adults.

Time: 1676 - 1686 **Age: 13-99**
ISBN 0-921100-64-7 **Can.$14.95 U.S.$12.90**

The Young Huguenots by Edith S. Floyer

It was a happy life at the pretty chateau. Even after that dreadful Sunday evening, when strange men came down and shut the people out of the church, not much changed for the four children. Until the soldiers came . . .

Time: 1686 - 1687 **Age: 11-99**
ISBN 0-921100-65-5 **Can.$11.95 U.S.$9.90**

The Shadow Series
by Piet Prins

One of the most exciting series of a master story teller about the German occupation of The Netherlands during the emotional time of the Second World War (1940-1945).

K. Bruning in *Una Sancta* about Vol.4 - The Partisans, and Vol. 5 - Sabotage:
. . . the country was occupied by the German military forces. The nation's freedom was destroyed by the foreign men in power. Violence, persecutions and executions were the order of the day, and the main target of the enemy was the destruction of the christian way of life. In that time the resistance movement of underground fighters became very active. People from all ages and levels joined in and tried to defend the Dutch Christian heritage as much as possible. The above mentioned books show us how older and younger people were involved in that dangerous struggle. It often was a life and death battle. Every page of these books is full of tension. The stories give an accurate and very vivid impression of that difficult and painful time. These books should also be in the hands of our young people. They are excellent instruments to understand the history of their own country and to learn the practical value of their own confession and Reformed way of life. What about as presents on birthdays?

Time: 1944-1945   **Age: 10-99**

Vol. 1 The Lonely Sentinel
ISBN 0-88815-781-9
Can.$7.95 U.S.$6.35

Vol. 2 Hideout in the Swamp
ISBN 0-88815-782-7
Can.$7.95 U.S.$6.35

Vol. 3 The Grim Reaper
ISBN 0-88815-783-5
Can.$6.95 U.S.$5.65

Vol. 4 The Partisans
ISBN 0-921100-07-8
Can.$7.95 U.S.$7.20

Vol. 5 Sabotage
ISBN 0-921100-08-6
Can.$7.95 U.S.$7.20